D0558869

MOURNING REDEMPTION

SHARON M. CLARKE
with illustrations by Sharon M. Clarke

Clarke Books
Anna Maria, Florida

Clarke Books

Copyright © 2006, 2007, 2008 by Sharon Clarke
All rights reserved. Published by The TRIAD Publishing Group
Previously published by Peppertree Press under ISBN: 0-9787740-6-x &
The TRIAD Publishing Group under ISBN: 978-0-9798244-8-7

No part of this publication may be reproduced, stored in a retrieval system, transmitted in any form or by any means, electronic, mechanical, photocopying, recording, or otherwise, without prior written permission of the publisher and author/illustrator.

ISBN 13:9781440439711
ISBN 10:1440439710
Library of Congress Number: 2006932895
Printed in the U.S.A.
Printed October 2008

THIS BOOK IS DEDICATED TO:

My Welsh-born husband Lyn, without whom I would never have traveled out of my own country to visit his.

To my parents, Homer and Patricia, for the fond memories of our family vacations revisiting our coal-mining roots in Pennsylvania.

To my daughter Danielle as well as her fiancé Lee for the thoughtful gift of a new computer and putting me online. The generosity.

Finally, to my youngest daughter Michelle, who has blessed me with two beautiful granddaughters, Brooke and Cailie, my life's joy.

ACKNOWLEDGEMENTS

The Waverley Encyclopedia.

The Civil War, an Illustrated History by Geoffrey C. Ward, with Rick Burns and Ken Burns.

Baseball, an Illustrated History by Geoffrey C. Ward and Ken Burns

Legends and Traditions of the Great War

Words, Expressions, and Terms Popularized 1914-1918

The World Wars

The Doughboys

Pershing's Doughboys WWI U.S. Army

Living History Group

Doughboy Center

The Story of the American Expeditionary Forces

The Big Show

The Meuse-Argonne Offensive: Part II

Pershing's Report, presented by The Great War Society

Website; Coal-mines early 1900's Pennsylvania; a collection of essays by Mr. David Kuchta, third generation coalminer - West Virginia Mine Wars.

one

ACROSS THE POND

The clouds were thickening with moisture as the Evans family boarded the ship bound for America. Once launched, they stood on the upper deck and watched as their old world disappeared from view. The clouds opened up and it had begun to rain in the distance. Rhodri understood that Mari was terrified of the uncertainty that awaited them. Getting a fair price for what little they owned was difficult enough. Mari felt as though each item was a piece of her own personal history. It was exceedingly bitter for her knowing that once she left her homeland she would never return again. Standing on the deck, she watched as the waves rolled back towards land and wished, in her heart, that she could jump ship and drift on a wave back to Wales. Her daydream came to a close when her husband Rhodri began to speak to her.

"Well would you look at that, Mari. Here we are high and dry and it is absolutely pissing down behind us. I take that as a good sign, don't you?"

Mari was not worried about signs. Her main concern was keeping an eye on their three sons amongst the throng of people aboard the ship which was no small task considering their ages. It seemed as though a year had passed since they sold the cottage and began their trek to America, when actually, it had only been about two and a half months earlier. They started their journey in their home town of Pontypool, Wales. From there, they made their way to Newport to catch a train bound for Fishguard where they were to take a ferry across the Irish Sea to Queenstown, Ireland. Neither Mari or Rhodri had ever been as far away from home as Ireland before. After disembarking the ferry, they then boarded the ship that would transport them across the Atlantic Ocean, all the way to Ellis Island into the New York Harbor. Nearing the end of their journey, they ran into some rough water. The ship heaved to and fro. Rhodri, Mari and most of the passengers became seasick and were heaving too. They left the lower berths, which was where they were assigned, to get some air. The ship's movement seemed worse down below, and the stench down there was enough to turn a pig farmer's stomach. They made their way to the viewing deck with their three boys who did not seem to be affected by the rocking and rolling of the ship at all. Geraint, their eldest son, saw an opportunity to have a bit of fun.

While Geraint's parents were seasick at one end of the ship, Geraint challenged Dafydd to a race. They quietly sneaked around the corner, away from their parents' watchful eyes. Then Geraint, knowing Morgan was too young to run the gauntlet, presented his little brother with an official position. He hoped that it would prevent him from feeling excluded from their game and keep him satisfied. Geraint informed Morgan that his main job was to stand at the far end of the ship and call who crossed the finish line first; his secondary job was to keep an eye out for their mother, who he thought would be mad as hell if she caught them running around. Geraint and Dafydd would race the entire length of the ship which was a daunting task considering the ship's movement on the undulating sea. Full concentration was needed to maneuver around the various obstacles that stood between them and their imaginary finish line. There were deck chairs strewn about; some were empty while others were temporarily occupied. The condition of the deck floor was an obstacle in itself. There were slippery areas where those who had become seasick during the voyage puked before they could make it to the rails. The boys also had to dodge the poor sick bastards who, with their hands cupped over their mouths, were rushing from their chairs desperately trying to make it to the rails. After a few races, Mari caught on to their little game. She heard some commotion on the deck and assumed it was her boys. She tried to muster enough strength to yell at Geraint to stop running around. She managed to warn them to stop or else she would break their necks just in case they failed to do it themselves. Their mother then turned and made her way back to the rail to join her husband; unfortunately, there were more fish for her to feed. Geraint went over to Morgan and, with malice, complimented him on his job of watching out for their mom.

"Good job, Morg."

Geraint watched as his mother made her way back around the corner and out of sight. He then insisted that Dafydd and he have one more race to determine a winner. Up till then they had completed two races, each winning one.

"Come on, boyo," Geraint taunted, "just one more to decide who's the world's best deck racer. Morgan, take your position, and this time keep your eyes peeled."

The determining race began. Dafydd had a good lead, but Geraint was not about to lose this race to his younger brother. He called out, "I've got yah now, boyo."

With that Dafydd turned to see the distance between them; he thought Geraint was about to overtake him. As he turned he tripped over a deck chair and fell arse over tits, sliding across the floor. He was covered in puke, and every other foul-smelling substance that covered the deck. Geraint was laughing so hard he thought his side would split. As Geraint crossed the finish line, he laughingly declared himself the winner and world-champion deck racer.

Dafydd called out, "No fair. Interference!"

"Interference my arse," Geraint exclaimed.

Dafydd protested, while Geraint, appearing to give in to his brother's protest, asked him if he wanted to have another race.

Geraint told him, "It's fine with me; we can do it again if you wanna take a chance on getting in more trouble. Hey, boyo, you don't have to worry about losing the race. When Ma gets a whiff of yah, she'll crown yah, all right."

Dafydd was so upset about the loss he had forgotten about the smelly state he got himself into. Geraint assured him that he would come up with some lie to tell their mother. They both threatened Morgan to keep his mouth shut, or else. Morgan was not sure what "or else" meant. He did have enough sense to know that he did not want to find out. Geraint told Dafydd and Morgan that as soon as they found their parents they were to sit perfectly still until Geraint could come up with a story. He instructed Dafydd to stay downwind of their parents. He did not want any extra attention being drawn to them. Rhodri and Mari felt like death itself. Neither of them paid much attention as to why the boys were suddenly there sitting like little angels. Mari was just relieved that they listened to her when she told them to stop running around. She turned to her husband in between heaves and asked if he thought their being so sick was a good sign. Rhodri was not up to a response but thought to himself that she must have been over the worst of it if she had the strength to be sarcastic. The boys were sitting there for over an hour when Dafydd looked towards Geraint for some guidance. By then everything that covered him from head to toe was dried, stiff and crusty. Geraint could not even look in his direction without bursting into laughter. Just then Morgan called to his parents.

"Look Ma, look! I can see her, I can see her!" he yelled out excitedly.

With those lovely words, their seasickness seemed to magically disappear.

Rhodri and Mari miraculously made it to their feet, and with their knees still shaking, patted their foreheads, cheeks and mouth with their sleeves in unison. Rhodri lifted Morgan up onto his shoulders so he could see above the crowd. It was Morgan's favorite place in the whole world. He knew nothing could ever harm him there. The Evans family tried to move towards the bow of the ship, but to no avail. The viewing deck was chock-a-block full with excited immigrants waving their little American flags. As the ship neared the Statue of Liberty, that great lady, standing tall with her torch stretched to the heavens in New York

Harbor, Rhodri was moved to tears. He knew it was the most awe-inspiring symbol that he would ever see. Mari just wanted off the ship and to plant her feet on dry land. As the family disembarked the ship, Mari placed her hand on Dafydd's shoulder to help guide him down the ramp.

"Duw, Dai, what in the world happened to yah, boyo!"

Geraint jumped in with the perfect answered for Dafydd.

"That lady back there threw up on 'im," he claimed pointing back into the crowd.

"Oh you poor dear. Don't yah worry. We'll get yah cleaned up," Mari said sympathetically.

Dafydd looked over at his brother Geraint with a sigh of relief on his pathetic face. Geraint felt completely chuffed by the acknowledgement of his fast thinking. He blamed the dastardly deed on a woman, knowing full well his parents would never want to further embarrass a lady by questioning her about the incident.

The pace of life in America was ten times faster than it had ever been back in Wales. Back in the old country, without exception, everyone had a routine imbedded in them from childhood. A person could tell what day it was and the time by who went where and what they were doing. Mrs. Dai Price would make her way to the market every morning, after stopping at Fugoni's Café for a cup of coffee, scones and a chat with Myfanwy Powell. The postman, Ianto Jones, delivered the mail early in the afternoon. He needed time to steam the letters open and read everything that was coming into the town. He felt it was his public duty, and no one could call him a slacker on that. If there was ever a bit of gossip you wanted to know, you just asked Ianto. He was more than eager to share his information and even embellish a bit if he didn't think the gossip was juicy enough.

On the rare occasion that there was a real medical emergency, everyone in town knew "The Collier's Arms" was where they could find Dr. Llewelyn, nursing a pint of Ansell's bitter ale while sitting in his favorite chair next to the fireplace. He knew all the children in the town by name as well as who their parents and grandparents were and where they lived. The town was like a jigsaw puzzle. Everything and everyone fitted tightly together into one scene that was repeated from generation to generation for as long as anyone could remember. The only thing that was changing in Pontypool was the mines were not producing as much coal as they had in the past. The mining company had begun down-sizing. Rhodri was one of many who was made redundant. That was one reason he left Pontypool to emigrate to America. In New York, everyone was rushing to and fro trying to eke out some kind of existence. They had no interest in knowing anything about you and avoided eye contact whenever possible. It was like being tossed from a reflecting pond into the churning white water of a fast-moving river. The native New Yorkers couldn't care less about your existence. They considered many of the immigrants to be less than human.

Rhodri and Mari decided that New York was not the place to rear the boys. They moved southwest and settled in a small town in Pennsylvania called New Salem. It lay nestled in the foot hills of the Allegheny Mountains, less than twenty miles from the West Virginia border. It was a proper coal-mining town. The Evans family was amazed by how much Pennsylvania looked like Wales, especially the area they chose to live in. Rhodri and the boys felt right at home the first time they laid eyes on the town. Rhodri went to work in the mines while they moved into the company housing that was set up for the miners and their families.

A heap of discarded slate was the town's landmark. It was only about a mile down the valley and stood about seventy feet tall. It did not matter where you stood in the town, whether you were in the patch or in the valley where the churches and businesses were, the great heap of slate was ever visible. A faint ominous vapor of smoke continually rose from the cracks at the top of the heap giving the illusion that it was volcanic and could erupt at any moment. The townies nicknamed it "Slate Dump Mountain." Directly behind the mound were the coke ovens, which looked like row after row of tiny brick igloos. Railroad tracks were woven throughout the countryside. The scent from the coke ovens enveloped the town year round. The ragamuffins that were raised there thought the whole world smelt of coal. Their whole world did.

Rhodri and Mari developed a daily routine reminiscent of the one they had back in Wales. As winter approached a thick gray fog bellowed from every chimney thickening the air and sky until, on some days, even the sun would be eclipsed by the smoke. New Salem was a typical American mining town. In Pontypool everyone was Welsh, but in the area where the Evans' now lived, there were many dialects. Each ethnic group took pride in the fact that they were now Americans, first and foremost, but they still enjoyed gathering into their cliques. Many of the miners would have a couple of drinks after a hard day in the pit. Whether you called The Gaslight a pub, a bar, a tavern, or a beer garden, that was where the miners met after their shift was over. There were other places to drink in town, but The Gaslight was directly across the road from the collier.

Where your family originally came from was not an issue for the men who worked in the mines. The miners were all on the same footing. Each of them worked hard for their wages. Most of the miners, along with their families, lived in company housing known as The Patch. They all shopped at the company store. The first thing a man was given when he hired into the mines was a tally number. In fact it was the only thing that was given to him. Everything else came out of their wages. The mining company automatically deducted anything that was owed to them before they received their pay package. They deducted the cost of renting the tools, including any wear and tear on them, and took a portion of what was owed to the company store. The men that worked the mines did backbreaking work, sometimes only receiving some change for wages at the end of the week. Because the company store extended credit to the miners and their families, the store could keep their prices high. There was not another store around that could compete financially with them.

The collier workers' families needed to use credit to make ends meet. By using the credit allotted to them, the miners became shackled to their jobs, always living in debt. Once you were heavily in debt, there was only one way out of the mines. That was with the help of six men; they were called pallbearers.

Miners went through a kind of metamorphosis. They entered the mines as men, but when they exited they looked more like a colony of moles. Getting coal dust in their eyes was inevitable in the pit. Between the irritation of the grit and the ever-present darkness, eventually all the miners suffered with poor eyesight. They also eventually suffered hearing loss. It was loud in the pit. The continual sound of a hundred men working their pickaxes extracting the coal from its fossilized existence echoed from shaft to shaft in no particular rhythm. It was just a lot of noise. Tensions were thick and the miners never knew when someone would call out the dreaded words, "CAVE IN!" Miners that worked for any amount of time had, more than likely, heard those words and watched as their friends and co-workers were buried alive beneath the weight of the coal and broken brace beams. The very sustenance that kept them and theirs alive was the very thing that could take their lives with only a cracking noise from a wooden brace to warn them. At least in a cave-in situation you would get a warning, no matter how slight. Poisonous gas and explosions could come without warning and were a constant threat. Coal dust was everywhere and under the right conditions could be highly volatile.

At the sound of shift's end, the colony of moles exited the tunnels. They were covered in coal dust, turning them blackish gray from head to toe, and from nostril to lung. Chances were that pneumoconiosis, commonly known as black lung, would more than likely get them in the end. It was a miserable way to eke out a living. Education was a luxury most people couldn't afford. If your education was lacking, as most men's were, a man's fate was either the mines or the steelworks. There weren't many other options for the uneducated to earn money in an industrial area. Whatever your father did for work, you did, and it did not take long before a boy was old enough to enter the workforce and contribute to the well-being of his family. The harder the times, the younger the boys.

The housing community on the hill, or the patch as the locals called it, overlooking the town, was row after row of the exact same houses. The floor plans were identical. The only distinction between them was how many steps you had leading to the front porch, which extended the full width of the dual family unit, the stairs being in the center. Some homes had no steps, while others had as many as fifteen, depending on the grade where the house was built. There was no class envy on the hill; no one was any better off than anyone else. The Evans's home had seven steps. Rhodri thought that was a good sign; he considered that seven was his lucky number. Each home was fueled by coal. The furnace was located in the cellar, tucked away under the stairs. It appeared to be a giant octopus coming out of the wall in the corner, beckoning for its next meal. Its colossal arms, the size of tree trunks, extended up through the ceiling to the upper floors. One furnace heated both homes. Each family had access to the furnace via a cast iron door on either side of the divided cellars. It's rotund base was half in the one home, the other half in the neighbor's. Morgan was terrified of it, and refused to go down, unless his mother went with him. His father had practically scared the life out of him the first time he went into the cellar. Rhodri saw the fear on Morgan's face the first time he laid eyes on the monstrous octopus lurking in the corner of the cellar and grabbed his shoulders and shook him saying, "It's gonna get yah," and that is all it took. Rhodri laughed like a drain. Mari, on the other hand, was furious with him for scaring Morgan like that.

Each home consisted of two rooms up and two rooms down. The bedrooms were located upstairs, while on the main floor they had their sitting room in the front facing the porch. The kitchen was at the rear of the home along with the stairs going up to the bedrooms or down to the cellar. The backyard was large enough for two clotheslines, one for each family. There was one outhouse for both families. It was, however, a two-seater, as long as your seats were small and you did not mind the company. The classic crescent moon was carved into the door. In the summertime after dinner, Rhodri would sometimes sit on the back stoop, with a bottle of beer to quench his thirst, and his twenty-two rifle. He liked taking potshots at the rats that ran through the alleyway behind the rows of outhouses. If Morgan and Mari were not around, he would sometimes allow Geraint and Dafydd to take a shot. They considered it quite a treat.

When the sun set, surrendering her light to the moon, Rhodri and the boys would watch as the squadrons of bats took to the skies for their evening missions. Mari continually warned the boys never to touch a bat or a rat, dead or alive, unless they wanted to get rabies. Morgan decided that he would prefer not getting rabies even though he had no idea what they were. Geraint and Dafydd knew what they were but never believed that they could get the disease simply by touching one. They had, more times than they could count, witnessed their father disposing of the rats that he had killed with his twenty-two, and as far as they could tell, he did not have rabies, or the black plague, which she too mentioned you could get by touching one.

October was a transitional month. The first week or so was usually warm during the daylight hours and cool after the darkness set in. Midway through the month the north winds would blow in and the days would grow shorter and colder. By November, all of the furnaces would be fully stoked. Thick, gray clouds of smoke bellowed from each and every chimney, filling the air with the pungent scent of coal. Families living on the hill often shared the task of the 4:00 a.m. feeding of the coal furnace in the cellar. Rhodri and Mr. Thompson worked out a schedule between the two of them. Each was responsible for every other morning. Heaven help you if it was your turn, and you failed in your duty by sleeping in. Both families would feel the chill as soon as they awoke in the morning, and the whole town would be informed of your infraction by afternoon. Nobody wanted the backhanded comments that would surely come his or her way. Once the furnace went out, it took a while to stoke it up again and even longer for the heat to reach the upper floors. No one liked the job, but it had to be done every morning during the winter months.

The first November that the Evans lived in New Salem, the boys came up with a scheme to earn some money. They wanted to purchase some fireworks to celebrate Guy Fawkes Day, or Bonfire Night as it was also called. It was a holiday they enjoyed every November back in the old country. They made a replica of Guy Fawkes and put it into a small box and placed it on the sidewalk in the town asking, "Penny for the Guy." Custom was, back in Wales, passers-by would drop a pence, or if you were lucky a shilling, in the box so you could buy some fireworks to blow up the box with the dummy in it on the fifth of November. In America the smallest coin was a penny, so that is what they decided to ask for. They did not earn a single cent, but what they did earn were quite a few strange looks. They had not realized that no one in America knew who Guy Fawkes was, and did not care that he had tried to blow up the House of Parliament. They were extremely disappointed as well as embarrassed and never tried the likes again.

One December morning Morgan came into his parents' bedroom complaining of being cold. He asked if he could crawl into bed with them. Mari took him back to the boys' room and placed him in between Geraint and Dafydd. Tucking him in, she assured him that he would be warm in no time and instructed him to go back to sleep, which he did. Mari went back to their room and nudged Rhodri.

"It's freezing in here. Is it your turn?" she asked not remembering.

Rhodri was half asleep an had to think for a minute. "No I did it yesterday," he grumbled.

"Well, are you going to see what's happened?" she said, nudging him again.

"Yes dear, I'll go see." He groaned not wanting to get out of bed.

It was still dark outside and very cold. Mari followed Rhodri downstairs with her shawl wrapped tightly around her shoulders. She told him that she would put the kettle on while he investigated. She lit the stove in the kitchen and began pumping the water into the tea kettle. Rhodri came in the back door after he tried checking on Mr. Thompson.

"That's queer. He's not there. I guess I'll have to go down and stoke the damn furnace."

"What do you mean, he's not there. He's gotta be there," Mari said with puzzlement in her voice.

"Mari, believe me, he's not there. Maybe an emergency came up. I don't know."

"I don't care what kind of emergency he might have had. He should have knocked the door. I swear, if Morgan gets pneumonia, I'll kill him with my own hands," she threatened.

Rhodri went into the cellar and took care of the problem. The fire had gone out just as they suspected. They sat in the kitchen, drinking their tea, discussing the mystery of where Mr. Thompson could have been. The heat slowly made its way throughout the house. The mystery was solved when Rhodri made his morning trip to the outhouse. He discovered Mr. Thompson's body crumpled over inside with his back flap down. It almost scared out of him the very purpose of the trip. He quickly used his neighbor's outhouse and returned for the body. He did not want his boys to see Mr. Thompson dead in the bog, referring to the outhouse. Rigor mortis had already taken place and he was having a heck of a time getting him out of the narrow door. Mari poked her head out the back door to see what was taking so long out there. She could see that he was struggling with something, but she could not make out what he was doing as it was still pretty dark outside. She came up behind him to ask if he needed some help.

"Jesus Mari, don't do that. You scared the shite out of me," he said as he dropped the body yet again.

"Duw, is that Mr. Thompson?" Mari said in shock.

"Aye, unless some other old man crawled into our crapper

and died last night. Let us just say he has had his last fart," he declared, as a matter of fact.

Rhodri asked Mari for some assistance. He was in an awkward position, and it was difficult to manage on his own.

"Come on Mari, help me get him in the house before the boys wake up."

"I don't want him in our house!" Mari exclaimed, not thinking.

Rhodri chuckled, "Duw Mari, not our house, his house."

"Oh," she said with some embarrassment.

They placed him on a chair in his kitchen, since he was already set in that position. They then placed a blanket over him, and went back to eat breakfast. Rhodri could not afford to be late for work. Mari planned on going into town and making the report after the boys left for school. Mr. Thompson was barely in the ground before the new neighbors moved in next door. The Hennessys emigrated from the village of Bally Teige in the county of Wexford. Three of their five children died and were buried back in Ireland. Sean Hennessy, along with his wife, Catherine, and their two daughters immigrated to America for work. They moved to New Salem so Sean could get a job in the coal mines. Kelly, their eldest daughter, was about the same age as Dafydd, and Ann, their youngest, was eleven months younger, being twelve years old.

Monday through Friday, just before sunrise, the miners quietly walked in the center of the road down the hill through the valley towards the mines. Barely a word would be spoken as they walked. Shift's end was another matter. The barman at The Gaslight watched the clock. A few minutes before the whistle blew, signaling the end of the day for the miners, he would start setting up the pints, two glasses deep the entire length of the bar. Then he would anxiously wait.

Within a few minutes of that blessed sound, which everyone longed for, he could hear the miners' shoes clogging in quick unison over the road and through the tavern's door. They bellied up to the bar and guzzled the first pint with such speed you would swear they did not have time to swallow. They would then slow down and savor the taste of their second pint that was sitting, pretty as you please, on the bar in front of them. Rhodri would stop at the tavern on occasion, but more often than not, he went straight home. Sean Hennessy had not missed a day at the tavern since he was hired. He always ordered a few, three, four, or more before he staggered home.

Rhodri looked forward to going home. He thought his boys were great fun and Mari was lovely. She was a comely woman. Her striking green eyes were complemented by her full lips set against her ivory complexion. Her long wavy chestnut brown hair was the summit of her petite frame. She kept her hair pinned up while she did her daily chores, usually to no avail. By midday strands of hair would work themselves free and be dangling about her face. She always tried to take the time to redo her hair and freshen up prior to Rhodri coming home. She wanted to look her best for him, and hated being caught looking untidy. She had a gracious manner about her, but she was staunch, especially with the boys. Rhodri, on the other hand, was playful, optimistic and a bit superstitious. Everyone enjoyed his company. He loved telling stories. He embellished when he thought that it was called for, but, for the most part, he was pretty accurate. His favorite stories were about his rugby days back in the old country. He claimed that he was so fast and thin back then that he could outrun his own shadow. He was average height, but always claimed he was a few inches taller than what he actually was. His boys figured that one out as they grew taller. Mari always knew he fibbed about how tall he was, but never let on that she knew. He had blonde hair and blue eyes, and was quite the lad. His first rugby coach thought that he was too thin to play the game effectively. He was afraid that he would snap like a twig the first time he was tackled. Rhodri's friends talked the coach into giving him a chance. His speed and agility won the coach over and got him a place on the team. He scored a try the first time on the pitch. He could sidestep and dummy a ball like nobody else. He was hurt before his first game was over.

A man on the opposing team was getting tired of seeing Rhodri running past him, so he clothes-lined him as he went racing by with the ball. He almost crushed Rhodri's windpipe. He had to be taken off the pitch for the remainder of the game. His throat was so sore after the game he was uncertain if he would be able to drink his pint, but he somehow managed to get it down. The young man that gave him the cheap shot ended up in the clubhouse too. He bought Rhodri a pint as a peace offering; of course, he gladly accepted the gesture. That young man, from that day forward, bought Rhodri a pint whenever there paths crossed. That is the way rugby was. They played the game with all of strength they could muster. Many times their adrenalin would get the better of them. After the match, they would put their aggression aside. Whatever happened on the pitch, stayed on the pitch. Retaliation waited until the next time the two of them met during their next game. Injuries were inevitable no matter what your size. Rhodri had his nose broken twice, both collar bones, dislocated his left shoulder, broke his right ankle and snapped his jaw in half. He maintained that breaking his jaw was the worst of all his injuries. His mouth was wired shut for six weeks. He thought that it was just as well that he could not eat during that period of time, because the thought of straining to take a shite would have been unbearable. The day they removed the wires he went to the nearest Chippy and ordered a meal. In fact he ordered three, one right after the other. The cook came out of the kitchen to get a better look at the emaciated young man that was eating his fish and chips like there was no tomorrow.

Regardless of all the pain and injuries he endured, Rhodri considered his days playing the game the best of his life, and the men he played, with and against, the best group of guys he ever knew or would ever know. He attributed meeting Mari to rugby. A friend of hers had a brother, Nobby Clark, that played with Rhodri on his team, which was called The Pontypool Harlequins. She went with her friend to see Nobby play. The first time her eyes clapped onto Rhodri running across the pitch she thought he was grand. She asked her friend to ask Nobby to introduce them at the workman's club dance that evening. All the rugby boys would be there after they ate and cleaned up. Mari wore her best outfit that night, and walked in with her friend Rhiannon, and her brother Nobby. They spotted Rhodri talking to Chalky White. They walked over for Nobby to introduce Mari, when Chalky turned around before Rhodri. As soon as he saw Mari, he asked her for the next dance. Her look of disappointment was apparent, but, out of courtesy, she graciously accepted. Chalky was a nice enough young man, but he looked like an unmade bed. Nobby explained to Rhodri, while Mari and Chalky were on the floor dancing, that Mari had asked about being introduced to him. Rhodri waited until the dance was about half over before he walked across the floor to cut in. He tapped Chalky on the shoulder, who reluctantly removed himself. Mari was never so happy to be interrupted. It was the last time Chalky, or any other man would hold Mari so close.

Rhodri and Mari were married within six months after their first dance at the workman's club. Nine months later Geraint was born; thirteen months later Dafydd came along. While Geraint and Dafydd were young, Mari's father became gravely ill. Rhodri, Mari and their young lads moved in with her parents to help out. Mari's mother Gladys was thankful and appreciated the company. She loved having the grandchildren around. While they were staying there Mari became pregnant for the third time. She was in her seventh month when her father passed away. When she gave birth, she and Rhodri had decided to name the child after her father. Morgana if they happened to have a girl and Morgan if the child was another boy. Gladys, Mari's mother, was pleased when Mari told her what they were planning to name their next child. She assured Mari that her father would have been very proud.

After the death of her father, they moved into their own cottage just down the street from her mother. Gladys came over every day to help Mari with the boys. They were growing so fast. She insisted that her house was too quiet now that Pa was gone.

She would really have liked Mari and the boys to move back in with her, but she never asked. She knew Rhodri needed to take care of his own family, just as her husband had for all those years. She was thankful for the months that they did live with her. Mari would have a pot of tea ready for her mother who would come over to visit them after Rhodri left for work.

One morning Rhodri and Mari were in the kitchen discussing the fact that many of the good miners were being made redundant. As they were talking, a blackbird somehow got into the house and flew through the kitchen. It startled the two of them. Rhodri knew it was a bad omen. As soon as he saw it, his first thought was, that bird is black as coal. He was afraid something awful was going to happen in the mines. A cave-in or an explosion, he did not know what, but he was sure something bad was about to happen. Mari told him that she thought his superstitions were a lot of nonsense, but the conversation stayed in the back of her mind the whole day and she prayed that nothing would happen to him. He went to work as he always had, knowing he could not let a little bird stop him from earning money for the family, but he was extra cautious that day and not as productive as usual.

Mari's mother stopped in just after he left for work, as she usually did. She told her mother about the bird incident and that she was a little concerned. Her mother said that a wild bird in the house was, indeed, a bad omen, and she did not blame Rhodri one bit for being afraid of going to work that day. She then proceeded to tell Mari horror stories about what had happened to this one and that one after a wild bird had gotten into their cottage. Mari was terrified by the end of their conversation. She told her mother that she was going to go down to the mines and get Rhodri the hell out of there. She asked if she could leave the boys with her while she went. Her mother calmed her back down and told her not to go running off half-cocked.

"He wouldn't need a cave-in to kill him. He would die of embarrassment if you ran down there. Duw Mari, what in the world would you say to his boss? 'I'm sorry Mr. Morrell, we saw a bird in our house today, so Rhodri has to come home now'?"

Mari rethought what she had considered and they changed the subject even though they both had it stored away in the back of their minds. Before her mother left that day, she took her wedding ring off and surprisingly gave it to Mari.

"Mari, I want you to take this ring and keep it safe. When Morgan's grown and decides to marry, have him use this ring. It would mean a lot to your father and me."

Mari was stunned. She had never in her life seen her mother take that ring off her finger. She accepted the ring with a few tears and assured her mother that she would treasure it until the day came that Morgan would marry. She looked at little Morgan's face and tried to imagine that one day her beautiful baby boy would be all grown up and wanting to marry. The gift touched her in a way she could not put into words. Her mother left, needing to go to market, but before she went on her way, she made sure that she gave Geraint and Dai a big hug and a kiss. She combed Morgan's hair out of his eyes, softly cupped his chin to give him a kiss, saying, "Look at that face; look at that lovely face." With that, she told them goodbye and left for the market.

Mari was never so relieved to see her husband walk through the door as she was that evening. They sat down, as a family, and ate their meal, enjoying every bite as though he had just escaped sure death. He had escaped, but not everyone was so fortunate. Mari's mother passed away unexpectedly in her sleep that very night. It was such a shock for Mari she was overtaken with grief. She cried for weeks, and stayed in a deep depression. Rhodri did not have the heart to tell her he had been made redundant at the mines. He decided a change of scenery would be good for his family, and, as far as he could tell, there was not anything or anyone to hold them in Wales anymore. He gathered all the money he had and purchased passage to America. He had not discussed his decision with Mari; he simply placed the tickets on the table in front of her when he came home that day. Mari was gobsmacked, but the sheer shock of what he had done snapped her out of her depression. He assured her that it would be a great adventure. They sold what they could not take with them, packed their bags, and left the old world behind to start anew. Rhodri and the boys adjusted quickly; however, for Mari, it took some time. She deeply felt the loss of her parents and now she was feeling the loss of her country too. Fortunately, she was far too busy during the day to dwell on it, and by evening, too tired to think about it.

Rhodri often thought of his days back in Wales, and the men he played rugby with. In his mind they would never grow up, or grow old, being frozen in time.

The Evans clan, unknowingly, moved to America during the West Virginia Mine Wars. The United Mine Workers of America, or the UMWA, had successfully organized Pennsylvania, Ohio, Indiana, and Illinois. Because of threats from The Baldwin-Felt Detective Agency, thugs hired by the mine owners to harass union organizers, the UMWA was unable to organize portions of West Virginia. The miners of Cabin Creek joined forces with their Paint Creek affiliates and made their demands which were fair and uncompromising:

1. The right to organize
2. Recognition of their Constitutional Rights to Free Speech and Assembly
3. An end to blacklisting union organizers
4. Alternatives to company stores
5. An end to the practice of using mine guards
6. Prohibition of cribbing (A wooden framed storage unit used to hold the coal. The coal producers estimated the weight in their favor.)
7. Installation of scales at all mines for accurately weighing coal
8. Unions being allowed to hire their own weighmen to make sure the companies' checked that weighmen were not cheating the miners from earned wages.

When the strike began, the Baldwin-Felt Detectives evicted all the miners and their families from company housing, forcing them to move into tents near the railroad tracks. The conditions of the tent city were appalling. Detectives were known to shoot their guns into the camp through the tents. The miners dug trenches within their tents for protection. The violent strike continued. An elderly woman, Mary Harris or "Mother Jones", Jones is a common Welsh name but Mary Harris was Irish. She was outspoken and adamantly stood in the workmen's corner. Mary lovingly referred to the miners as "her boys." February 7, 1913, an armored train, The Bull Moose Special, as it was nicknamed, stopped in front of the miners' camp. The doors opened, revealing its deadly passengers. The Baldwin-Felt Detectives opened fire with their machine guns into the tents. Amazingly, only one of the miners, Cesco Estep, was killed. A few days later Mother Jones was arrested for inciting a riot. The violent struggle continued for years. Miners that worked in the North, although not effected by the War, empathized with their fellow miners in West Virginia. News of the conflict only made the newspapers when extreme violent acts were committed, but it was a burden that all miners cared about deeply.

two

FRIENDSHIP

Rhodri woke prior to the five-thirty alarm. There was a chill in the room. Mari insisted that they slept with the window ajar for the fresh air. He did not mind as long as his wife was there to help ward off the cold. That particular morning, he rolled over to cuddle up to her warmth as he did every morning when he was cold, but to his surprise, she was not there. He got up and went down the stairs to investigate. Mari was at the stove preparing their breakfast, but she was obviously preoccupied. Her hands and body were moving as though she were in a heated debate. He was not sure who was winning the argument, Mari one or Mari two, seeing that there was not another soul around. Rhodri decided to allow her to carry on with her conversation as he went to retrieve the newspaper from the front porch. Mari was so engrossed she had not noticed him walking through the kitchen. She heard the front door close as he was coming back inside.

She looked puzzled. "Where were you?"

"I guess I could ask you the same question, now couldn't I?" was his response.

She was already on edge, so when he answered her question with a question, it upset her. He could tell by her face that he was pushing his luck, and quickly changed the subject. He asked if his morning tea was ready yet. She set it in front of him without saying a word, slipping back into her trance. He read the paper and drank his tea, oblivious to anything around him, until he could smell his breakfast burning.

"Mari," he called to her from the table.

As soon as she heard her name she snapped out of it, and removed the pan from the burner. She apologized for the state of his breakfast.

"Ah, I'm sure it'll be fine. A little black won't hurt me. Hell, I swallow coal dust all day long for a living. Do you want to talk about it?" he asked, not really having much time to get into a lengthy discussion. She gave a deep sigh and was about to tell him what was on her mind, when Geraint came running down the stairs, stopping her cold. He grabbed a piece of toast from the table and went out the back door to the outhouse. Rhodri asked again. She assured him that it was not life-threatening and that they would be able to talk about it after he came home from work. She told him that it was a private matter, and that she did not want to discuss it in front of the children. She gave him a kiss and handed him his canteen and lunch pail and sent him off to work. Dafydd was the next to come charging down the stairs, as though a vicious dog were at his heels.

"Slow down," she called out as he ran out of the back door.

There was no slowing him down. He ran into the outhouse and almost jumped in right on top of Geraint.

"Hang on, boyo. I'm done," exclaimed Geraint. Their bodies shifted around each other to get to their respective places, Geraint wanting out and Dafydd desperately needing to get in. When Geraint came back into the kitchen, Mari inquired if Morgan was up yet.

"Who am I, my brother's keeper?"

"Don't get smart with me, Cain, I mean Geraint," she snapped back, not appreciating the tone he used when answering her.

"Sorry Ma. I couldn't help it. No, he was still asleep when I came down," Geraint said apologetically.

Just as they were speaking, they could hear Morgan making his way down the stairs. She gave him a kiss and sat him down at the table to eat. Dafydd came in and was also ready to eat. She placed their breakfast on the table.

"It's burnt!" exclaimed Geraint.

"It's not that bad. Your father ate it. Just scrape off the

black and eat it." his mother told him.

Geraint and Dai were so hungry they ate it without further complaint and left for school. She made herself another cup of tea and sat with Morgan as he finished his breakfast. The sun had come up, but the February sky was overcast and gray, just like her mood. When Rhodri came home from work he asked if she was ready to tell him what was troubling her. Unfortunately, it was Friday, which meant it was bath night. As soon as their supper was finished and the dishes were washed, it was time to begin heating the water for their bath. Geraint and Dai went into the cellar to carry the tub up to the kitchen. The routine was Rhodri would bathe first, then the eldest boy, followed by Dai, then Morgan being the youngest, was always the last to bathe. People used to use the phrase, "Don't throw the baby out with the bath water." That was because the water would be so filthy for the baby's bath, you could easily lose sight of them in the tub. By the time their Friday night ritual was completed, it was time for the boys to go to bed. Mari would bathe when no one was around enjoying her clean water and her privacy. She walked them up the stairs and tucked the blankets around them, telling them goodnight. When she came back down the stairs, she was tired and did not feel like talking about anything. Rhodri insisted that she tell him. She was not sure how to start, even though she had thought of nothing else all that day. She stalled for a moment, searching for the right words.

"My visitor's a few months late," she softly told him.

A puzzled look came over his face as though she were speaking in code. As far as he knew they were not expecting anyone. She knew what he was thinking and rolled her eyes in disbelief.

"You know..." she said with a whisper and clenched teeth.

Her hormones were raging, and she was getting ready to follow their lead. He was still wondering who was coming over.

"Duw Rhodri, I'm pregnant!" she exclaimed.

"Is that all? Jesus, Mari, for a moment I thought it was

something serious," he said relieved.

"It is serious. If my mother was here, I wouldn't mind so much, but I don't have anyone to help me now," she complained as her eyes began welting up with tears.

"Luv, calm down. I'll help you," he said, trying to console her.

"How the hell do you think you're going to help me? If you're not at work, you're off playing baseball, or outside shooting rats. What kind of help is that?" she smarted off becoming angry at his suggestion.

He became defensive knowing that she was right. "Well, maybe this time you can have the baby in a real hospital instead of at home?"

"A hospital? Jesus, Rhodri, they're as high as cats' backs. You know we cannot afford that. It's not that anyways. You do not understand how full my hands are now. You have no idea how much work a new baby will be for me," she insisted.

"Ah, don't you worry; everything will come out in the wash," he said making light of her concerns.

"The wash, oh my God, all that washing," she said with a deep sigh.

Rhodri put his arms around her and said, "Worry not, Luv, I'll be there for yah. After all, I was obviously there when it counted," he chuckled.

As soon as he saw the look on her face, he went on to Defend. "Hey, I was only poking at you in fun. You didn't have to take me serious."

Her jaw dropped while she raised her hand, and for a split second, thought about slapping the grin off of his smug face.

"Yeah, laugh now, funny man. In a few months when you'll really want a poke, see if you get one. What will you do then?" she sneered.

He looked at his right hand, and while moving his wrist back and forth, declared that he would be just fine. His rude joke had cut the tension and made her laugh.

"Duw, what a wanker," she said with a smile, shaking her

head in disbelief.

They looked at each other and both began to laugh. They decided that it was late and they needed to turn in for the night.

Rhodri jokingly inquired on their way up the stairs, "I guess a poke is out of the question, aye."

"You can bet your life on that one, boyo," she said adamantly.

With that remark out of the way, they went to bed. Mari was relieved that she was able to confide in Rhodri about her concerns with having another baby. She hoped that all she needed was a good night's sleep.

As the months rolled on, the unrelenting cold winter was taken over by a cold, wet spring. The rainy days just gave Mari the blues. Even small things overwhelmed her. It was now April and Mari's birthday was only a week away. Rhodri hoped that he could lift her spirits by surprising her with a small party. He splashed out and ordered a cake from their local bakery to be picked up on the thirteenth, Mari's birthday. He planned on hiding the cake in the cellar until after supper and then surprising her with it. The boys were excited about the party and promised not to say a word about it. They gathered together some change and went to the Five and Ten Store to buy their mother a gift. The boys were very proud of what they were able to buy for her. Miss. Slattery, the lady that worked at the store, helped the boys choose something nice. They went so far as to wrap it in a clean handkerchief and tied it up with a ribbon, making it look quite presentable. After their evening meal was over, Rhodri asked Mari to go into the sitting room and put her feet up, while he and the boys cleaned up the kitchen.

Mari protested, "You and the boys, clean the kitchen? I think I'd rather do it myself, thank you very much."

Rhodri insisted, "Not another word. Now get in there and relax. We'll call you as soon as we've finished."

She left the room grumbling that they had better not break anything, and decided to go ahead and let them try. She could always go back behind them and redo everything the next day if needed. She went into the sitting room and worked on some mending that was folded in a basket next to her chair. She kept her ears tuned in for the sound of breaking glass, but she didn't hear anything out of the ordinary. Rhodri had worked out a plan to make everything go smoothly. He placed a chair near the counter for Morgan to stand on so he would not feel left out.

"OK boyos, let's do a good job for your mom. I'll scrape and hand you the dishes for washing," he told Geraint.

"Dai, you'll be the rinse man," he said giving him his appointment.

"And Morgan, you can help me dry and put the dishes away, because, my little boyo, I have no idea where this stuff goes. Can yah do it?" he asked, as though it were the most important job of the task.

"Sure I can, Daddy. I know where everything goes," said Morgan.

"Good man. OK boyos, let's get cracking but not the dishes."

Rhodri pumped the water into the sink for Geraint and Dai. The project ran like a well-oiled machine. They had everything done in no time. Rhodri retrieved the cake from the cellar and placed it on the table along with some clean plates and forks. He asked the boys to stand in front of the table so their mother would not be able to see the surprise. Rhodri called Mari back into the kitchen. She marveled that they had finished so quickly. She just knew that in that amount of time they could not have done a proper job of it. This she had to see for herself. She came into the kitchen and, as she neared the table to see what kind of job they had really done, the boys moved, revealing the cake, and called out, "HAPPY BIRTHDAY."

Mari was stunned; her eyes filled with tears and she began to cry.

Rhodri went over and kissed her on the cheek, "All for you, my luv."

"I can't believe you remembered; I forgot myself. Is today

really my birthday?" she questioned.

Geraint cleared his throat, interrupting them. He wanted to turn her attention to the cake that was sitting on the table uncut.

"Yes Geraint, I see the cake; it's lovely," she said noticing how nicely it had been decorated for her.

The boys did not care how lovely the cake was; they just wanted to dig into it. Rhodri cut the cake and gave Mari the first slice.

"What a lovely surprise. I can't believe you boys did all this for me. And you, Morgan," she said pointing her finger at him smiling. "You knew about this and didn't let on." Her little boy was growing up.

He grinned with pride over the acknowledgement that even he could keep a secret. Before Mari could finish her cake, the boys were giving her the gift they picked out.

She put her plate down. "Presents too? Ah, you boys didn't have to do this. Doing the dishes was gift enough for me."

Geraint nudged Dai. "See, I told yah."

Mari carefully untied the ribbon and commented that she would use it for her hair. She looked at the bottle that they had nicely wrapped, not knowing for sure what it was. She opened it to see if it had a scent to it. "Is that lilac I smell?"

"It's oil for your hands," chirped Morgan.

She tipped the bottle with her finger over the opening and applied a dab to the back of her hand. "Ooh, it smells lovely; don't I feel like the Queen of Sheba. It's a wonderful gift and a wonderful surprise. Thank you so much."

It was the nicest birthday she had ever had. She gave each of them a hug and a kiss as she unsuccessfully fought off some tears. They had a grand time, and retired to the sitting room, where Rhodri regaled them with stories about his old rugby days. Morgan had fallen asleep, cuddling up next to his mother on the settee. She then announced that it was time for bed. Geraint and Dafydd began to protest at their mother's directive, but their father immediately ended the uprising with merely a look. They gave their mother a good night kiss and went to bed. Rhodri carried Morgan up the stairs. He told the boys to be quiet and go to sleep. He wasn't half way down the stairs before he could hear Geraint and Dai cutting up. He had a feeling that the cake and stories would wind them up, making it hard for them to go to sleep that night.

Rhodri called back up, "Quiet or I'll get the belt."

Silence. Nothing strikes fear into the heart of a child as much as those dreaded words. Rhodri had only whipped the older boys one time. They never forgot it and they never wanted it to happen again. When they first moved to New Salem the town was still reeling from the story of poor Little Ben Bauer. Rhodri and Mari shared the story with their boys to stress to them the importance of just how dangerous playing near the railroad tracks were. Some local children had been jumping onto moving freight cars for fun. Little Ben Bauer wanted to give it a try. He was the youngest of the group, being only eleven years old. The other children there were fourteen and fifteen. All of them had been warned never to play near the railroad tracks. Little Ben slipped as he jumped and lost his grip, which caused him to miss the open door of the boxcar and slide under the train. He lost both of his legs just below his knees. The local children panicked and ran off, leaving him there by himself. The train authorities found his legless body the next day about twenty feet from the tracks. The official's concluded that he must have tried to drag himself home, but did not have the strength to make it very far. He bled to death not a mile from his house. Not one of the children involved told their parents what had happened to Ben. After the body was found, one by one, they began ratting each other out until all involved confessed. The town was heartsick. Still, after knowing all of that, Geraint and Dai ignored their parents' warning and went down to the tracks to play. Mr. Taylor, the father of one of the children that was present when Little Ben Bauer lost his life, chased Geraint and Dafydd off and told their father what they were up to. Rhodri was both furious as well as highly disappointed in the two of them. The disappointment on their father's face hurt worse than the actual whipping that they received. The town buried the story with Little Ben Bauer. Nobody wanted to be reminded that their own children could do something so cowardly. The guilt from that awful event would live forever in the hearts of the families involved.

The day after the birthday party, Mari was at the stove getting their tea ready as Rhodri stepped out to retrieve the daily news report. He hadn't unrolled the paper to see the headline until he had his tea in front of him.

"Oh my God, Mari, the Titanic sank," he burst out with disbelief in his voice.

"Duw, it can't be. I thought it was unsinkable," she marveled at the headline.

The news about the British liner was horrific. Details of the disaster were forth coming. Every day more and more was known about the tragedy. Everyone in town was affected, but no one was affected more than their new neighbors, the Hennessys. Catherine's parents were on the Titanic that fateful day, although they did not know it when first reported. Neither of them survived. There were twenty-two hundred people that booked passage, from the very wealthy to the dejected of society. A few of the lost wealthy were Jacques Futrelle, a famous French novelist and J.J. Astor, who traded furs with the Indians and made his wealth purchasing land in New York. Among the little known poor immigrating were Pat and Alma Doyle, Catherine Hennessy's parents. They were bringing everything they owned with them. It was to be the Titanic's maiden voyage. Before she sailed, the papers boasted that God himself couldn't sink her, and she was deemed unsinkable. In reality, all it took was a single iceberg.

Articles about the last moments on board the Titanic were surreal. The hundreds of families in the lower berths never had a chance, and they knew it. That was where Pat and Alma Doyle were thought to have been when the ship sank. On the viewing deck, the band continued to play even after the last of the lifeboats was lowered into the water. The last song they played was the hymn, Nearer My God to Thee. As soon as the last note sounded the ship reportedly tipped, plunging the band members and everyone else on board into the freezing water. In an instant, that majestic ship that was thought unsinkable, alas, was gone. She slipped beneath the waves never to be seen again, taking one thousand five hundred souls with her, enveloped forever in the arms of Poseidon. The only passengers that did survive were the fortunate ones that made it into the lifeboats. Everyone that ended up in the sea died of hypothermia before they could be reached. There was a ship nearby called Carpathia. Those in the lifeboats were rescued quickly after the disaster. Many of those that did survive were in shock, not believing what they had just witnessed. Crew members of the Carpathia tirelessly searched for anyone trying to hold on to a piece of the wreckage to survive. The crew found the ocean was eerily silent after the Titanic sank. No one called out for help. No one called at all. Seeing all of the lifeless bodies floating gently in the water looked to some of the crew as though they could walk in any direction without their feet touching the water, moving from one human isle to another. Everyone was touched by the story.

A couple of weeks after the ship sank, Catherine Hennessy, the Evans' neighbor, received a letter from her mother telling her that they were coming. She had no idea that her parents were on their way to America via Titanic. When the passenger list was finally published, Catherine searched for her parents' names; her greatest fears were confirmed. She was devastated. Mari could hear her sobbing through the walls. She empathized, having lost her parents prior to coming to America. Mari decided that she would make a meal for the Hennessyes and take it over. She prepared a pot of stew as well as made a loaf of freshly baked bread. Catherine was touched by her kindness. Mari allowed a week to pass before she went back to see how Catherine was faring. She remembered how devastated she was after her loss and would not have wanted to entertain strangers right away. She decided to wait and make a call on Mrs. Hennessy during the next coal miners' baseball game. She knew on those days, everyone that could go, would go. Whether they were a player or just a spectator, they would be busy at the diamond. Rhodri had informed Mari that Sean Hennessy, Catherine's husband, had joined the New Salem miners' team and would be playing in the next game. She didn't think that Catherine would want to be in the middle of a crowd just yet, and would more than likely stay at home. She was right. Geraint and Dai went to watch their father play, so it was only she and Morgan left at home. They went over and knocked Catherine's front door. Ann Hennessy, the youngest of the Hennessy's daughters, saw them through the screen door, and without inviting them in, called for her mother who was in the backyard hanging up laundry. Mari stood on the porch until Catherine came to the door and invited them into her home, apologizing for Ann's bad manners. Mari, in turn, apologized for taking her away from her chores. Catherine explained that she could use the break and asked Kelly, her eldest daughter, to go out and finish hanging the clothes on the line for her. She invited Mari to join her for a cup of tea.

Catherine looked over at Morgan and sighed, "Ah, my Aemon was about your age. It's too bad he's not here to play with you."

Catherine asked Mari if she would not mind Ann keeping an eye on Morgan outside. The suggestion was fine with Mari. Ann came down and took Morgan in the backyard where Kelly was hanging the laundry. She grabbed a couple of tins from the cupboard to use as buildings and a couple blocks of wood to be used as trucks. Morgan thought it was great fun playing with Ann, and developed a huge crush on her from that day forward.

"It's such a nice day, he shouldn't be cooped up in the house listening to us nattering on," claimed Catherine, referring to Morgan. "And besides, I know that Ann misses playing with her baby brother, Aemon."

Catherine proceeded to tell Mari about the loss of three of her children back in Ireland, and how tragic it all was. She also told her she was never so glad to leave a place as she was when they left Ireland. They enjoyed their cup of tea and talked as though they had known each other their whole lives. They talked about their journey to America. Mari told her about the loss of her parents and how difficult it was for her. That, and Rhodri having been made redundant at the mines, prompted their move to America. Catherine told Mari that they also moved because of a lack of work and the fact that they had already lost three of their babies over there. Two of her girls, Emma and Margaret, died of consumption, and her third child and only boy, Aemon, fell to his death from one of the cliffs that they lived near. Mari marveled at the amount of misery she had endured and now she had lost her parents too. They spent the entire afternoon comforting each other, but by now they could hear the townies coming down the road.

"Well, by the sounds of it, the game's over. I better go home and finish their meal. I cut the boyos a plough man's lunch to take to the game. I'm sure that's worn off by now," Mari said excusing herself.

She thanked Catherine for the tea, called for Morgan and went home. Catherine was glad that she had taken the time out of her busy day to get to know her neighbor a bit. It helped her to be able to talk about her loss. She had confessed to Mari that she found it difficult to express her feelings to Sean, and that he was not a sympathetic person. Mari had a hard time believing some of the comments Catherine had made about her husband, Sean. He seemed sincere, happy, and was always smiling. In fact Mari was of the opinion, before their little chat, that Catherine was the one that seemed standoffish, not Sean. Before that day, Catherine kept to herself, not looking in Mari's direction when they would pass each other in town while marketing. She even seemed to avoid her when doing household chores. Mari found that as soon as she came inside from hanging out her laundry, Catherine would then make her way outside to do hers, but never while Mari was in the yard. It made Mari uncomfortable starting a conversation with her. After the boys had gone to bed, Mari asked Rhodri what he knew about Sean Hennessy. He told her that he was a good worker, and in his words, "a hell of a good first baseman."

The Hennessys had only lived in New Salem a little over four months. They moved next door the end of December, just after Mr. Thompson died in the outhouse. That particular winter had been especially cold, so Mari really had not seen much of her new neighbors. She thought that maybe she just misunderstood some of what Catherine had said to her. In the weeks to come, Catherine and Mari talked often. She came to realize just how wrong her first impression was. Catherine was not standoffish at all. As a matter of fact Mari found her kind, loving, thoughtful, and funny. She feared her husband's unexpected outburst, which, she had confessed to Mari, happened frequently. Catherine said she felt like she and her girls had to walk on eggshells whenever he was around, and that he was like two different people living in one body. The one Sean Hennessy was a smiling, sincere, happy-go-lucky kind of guy; that Sean Hennessy was used for public viewing. The other Sean Hennessy only showed his true colors in front of his "so called" love ones; he was the Sean Hennessy that only came out in the private. In Catherine's opinion, that was the true Sean Hennessy; the other one was a hypocrite.

The spring rains had washed away all remaining remnants of the coal dusted grayish black snow. It was not as rainy as it had been the month before, but the land was still spongy with water. The air was fresh and renewed, being warm most days, but still briskly cold after the sun went down. The spring flowers were in full bloom and so was Mari. Fortunately, she and Catherine had become thick as thieves. They enjoyed a cup of tea and a chat on their front porch nearly every weekday while their husbands were at work. From there they could easily hear the shifts whistle or the school bell. This arrangement worked out especially well for Catherine. She told Mari that if Sean were to come home and catch either her or the girls sitting around and not working when he had been, there would be hell to pay.

She told Mari about the time, just after they had moved to New Salem, when Sean came in and caught Kelly and Ann playing jacks in the sitting room. They had both finished their chores and homework and asked if they could play. The house was shut up tight because of the cold, so they could not hear the whistle signifying shift's end, and besides that he always went to pub after work. Catherine said that she was busy in the kitchen and that she and the girls lost track of the time. When Sean came home and saw the girls enjoying themselves, he went into a rage. He kicked the jacks everywhere while grabbing Kelly and Ann by their hair. He dragged them through the scattered jacks lying all over the floor and into the kitchen to confront their mother. They rose to their feet crying. He screamed at them to get up to their room and kicked at them as they ran up the stairs crying. He maintained that his complaint was, "How dare you let them lazy brats play while I'm busting my arse working!" He would carry on and on late into the evening. She explained to Mari that whenever she would try to intercede for the girls, he would simply turn his venomous tongue on her, which she preferred. She would rather have him attack her than her girls. He had also told Catherine that on that particular night the girls were not allowed to come down to eat. He faulted them for not contributing to the well-being of the family. He then went on to name call, and blame her for everything that was wrong in their lives, including the deaths of their three children. Catherine said that when he got his dander up there was no stopping him. He would continue the argument for days on end. The things he would say to Catherine and the girls, in Mari's opinion, were beyond cruel. Catherine maintained that he was strong as an ox and twice as stubborn.

Their friendship lifted both of their spirits. Mari was able to talk to Catherine about her fears concerning having another baby, while Catherine, or Cate as Mari now called her, was able to share what really went on behind closed doors with Sean. Mari was now confident that Cate would be there for her when the time came, just as her mother was back in Wales.

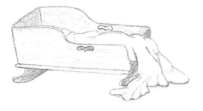

three

LABOR OF LOVE

Spring was coming to a close and summer was fast approaching. Everyone had their windows open to allow the summer breeze to keep the house cooled off. The Evans family could now easily hear Sean ranting and raving at his family, but as soon as he walked outside, that smile, which he was known for, was plastered on his face. He walked around as though he were running for office and needed your vote. It about made Mari ill. She could not understand how Cate put up with it. She knew she would never have put up with that kind of behavior, but for her friend's sake, Mari acted as though she never heard the yelling. Living next to them helped Mari to appreciate her life with Rhodri even more. Cate told Mari that when she made her vow before God and the church, she meant it with all her heart, and that she would never break her commitment, being a strict Protestant. She told Mari that it was not God's mistake, it was hers, and that she had no choice but to live with it.

Cate confided in Mari about everything, including things she never shared with even her pastor. It was a wonderful vent for her. She told Mari about the many times she would wake in the middle of the night only to find Sean standing at the foot of the bed staring at her, mumbling to himself that he was not going to live like this anymore. It really frightened her. She told Mari that when that would happen she would go downstairs and try to sleep on the sofa, but the moment she could relax enough to drift off, he would always come down and order her back to their bed. She said that it was unnerving to say the least. Cate and the girls would try their best not to set him off, but his behavior was so absurd and erratic there was no way they could avoid his wrath. Cate told Mari that the only endearing name she could bring herself to call him was "Hun," but that she was always thinking "Attila." Mari asked Cate how in the world she could ever have sex with the likes of him, knowing how he treated her and the girls.

Cate's response was, "Sex. You know, Mari, it's the oddest thing. When we first met and were just courting he was all over me all of the time, like a randy octopus. He would get so frustrated, but sure enough, as soon as I said 'I do,' and would, he completely lost interest. At that time, as hard as it is to admit now, I really wanted to do it, and I mean every night. I was young, stupid, in love, and married. After the first night, he didn't want anything to do with it. He made me feel dirty, cheap and sinful. It was horrible. I couldn't go to my pastor and tell him these things. I had to figure it out for myself, and I finally did. It was all a game to him. I know how he thinks now. As soon as he realized that I might actually like it, he decided it was a sin. Unless he wanted to do it; then it was all right. Now that I can't stand the thought of him touching me, guess what, he has a renewed interest. I swear the man is trying to drive me around the bend. Thank the Lord he's fast. That's if he can do it at all. The drink, yah know, makes his wedding tackle limp."

Mari was laughing uncontrollably while the tears streamed down her cheeks. She found that Cate could turn the worst situation into the funniest story. She could not imagine how she kept her humor through it all.

Cate went on to confess, "I probably shouldn't tell you this," she said starting to blush. "It's such a sin."

"What is?" Mari asked still laughing.

"Sean thinks I like it on top."

Mari claimed, "I could be wrong, but I really don't think that's a sin."

"Well it probably is in the church's eyes, but that's not what I'm talking about." Cate made the sign of the cross, kissing her fingers afterwards. "No, I can only do it on top because I imagine that I'm suffocating him with my breast," Cate stared in a matter of fact way.

"Aye, you're probably right about that being a sin," Mari concurred.

"Can you picture me confessing that to my pastor?" Cate chuckled.

By this time Mari and Cate were laughing so hard again tears were running down both of their faces. Mari begged for mercy. She warned Cate that if she kept telling her such things she would send her into labor early. She still had approximately six weeks left to her pregnancy. The antics of Attila would come up often as they sat on the porch enjoying their tea time, but they were now concentrating on making some preparations for the new arrival. Cate suggested that she talk to Dr. Pritchard to let him know they may be needing him soon. Mari assured Cate that Dr. Pritchard knew when she was to deliver and that she never needed a doctor before and did not expect that she would need one now.

"Trust me, Cate. I've had three healthy boys without a doctor's help, and I expect this one will be another healthy boy," she said patting her tummy.

"And besides, Dr. Pritchard is fully aware just how far I am along. If anything happened, God forbid, I'll send Rhodri or one of the boys to fetch 'im. You don't have to worry. I'll be fine, you'll see."

Mari could hardly believe what was coming out of her mouth. She sounded just like Rhodri, but she was confident, that between the two of them, they could handle everything. Mari had fresh towels and linens set aside in a cradle that her father made when Geraint was born. For Mari, the cradle had great sentimental value. Whenever she touched it, she thought of her father and how proud he was to make it for her. All three of her boys slept in it when they were little, and now her fourth child would too. It was the only piece of furniture she insisted that they bring with them. Mari could not imagine leaving it behind.

Friday came around and as usual their afternoon tea was in full session. They were sitting on the porch talking about this, that and Attila, when they heard the final school bell toll. Mari gave Morgan permission to wait at the end of the path for Geraint and Dai. It took a few minutes before you knew the children were coming up the hill. You could hear them before you could actually see them. There was still no sign of the boys as Kelly and Ann came up the front path. Ann said a simple "hello" to Morgan as she passed him. He was so embarrassed he just stood there looking as though he could not speak. His mother called out to him and instructed him that it was rude of him not to speak when he was spoken to, and to answer her. Still no response was given. His eyes rolled back in his head as though he would faint; he had such a huge crush on her. As Ann walked up onto the porch, Mari apologized for Morgan, whispering to her that he was in love. Ann began to blush a bit and nodded her head acknowledging that she knew. But then everyone knew; it was so obvious. Mari had finished her cup of tea and gathered Morgan to go inside and finish their supper. Still there was no sign of the boys. Cate too had chores that she needed to catch up on before Sean came home. She knew full well that she and the girls had better busy themselves with something before he came up the path. Geraint and Dai finally came running into their kitchen about a half hour late. They were both excited and apologized, explaining that there was a fight after school and that they had to stay to see who won.

"Who was fighting?" Mari asked.

"Tommy Dunn and Orville Jenkins," both Geraint and Dai said in unison.

"Well I guess I should have known a Jenkins would be involved. Why were they fighting?" she asked.

They shrugged their shoulders, not knowing what had started the fight.

"Ah Ma, yah should have been there. Tommy gave Orville a bloody nose and everything," informed Dai.

"Well, well, as much as I would have liked to have seen Orville get his, I've got things to do, and by the way, so do the two of you. Bath night, you know."

The look of disappointment washed over their faces faster than they could have used a face cloth. They both wanted desperately to go back to see what did start the fight. Their mother would have none of that. They would have stayed, but they were all chased off by Mr. Langdon, the local butcher.

They begged their Mom to let them go see Tommy after supper.

"Forget it. You'll only end up in trouble. Mr. Langdon's already chased you off once. Do you want your father to find out about this?" she reasoned.

"Ah come on, Ma. Pleassssse. With sugar and spice and a cherry on top," begged Dafydd.

"Absolutely not, and not another word or I will tell your father."

Geraint wished she would tell. "He'd let us go. He'd probably go with us," he grumbled under his breath.

"Don't the two of you have homework? You can always find out what started it tomorrow. Now get going," she insisted.

They admitted that they did have some, but with it being the weekend, they felt they had plenty of time to get it done. But, their mother still insisted that they go to their room and do their homework before supper. She also reminded them again that it was bath night. Dai knew when he was licked. He also knew that if they kept it up she might send them out to fetch a switch to be used in a most disagreeable way. They could even be jeopardizing their attendance to Saturday's baseball game, if their mother was so inclined. And they surely did not want to do that. Still they dropped their shoulders and Geraint grumbled again as they dragged themselves up the stairs as though they would never see the sunshine again.

"Tomorrow, we could be dead tomorrow," Geraint mumbled within ear shot of his mother.

Mari chuckled as she called up to them, "Well at least you'll die clean and educated."

Mari put the finishing touches to their meal. She was making Rhodri's favorite, gammon, mashed potatoes and gravy, with mushy peas. She had also baked a loaf of fresh bread. Everything was near ready, so she hurried up the stairs to freshen up before Rhodri came home. She was coming down the stairs and met him in the kitchen. He told her that he could smell the aroma from the front porch. He set his lunch pail down on the small counter near the sink and inquired if he had forgotten a birthday or anniversary. She assured him that he had not.

"No, silly. I just felt so good today. I thought I would surprise you with your favorite dinner," she reported happily.

"And what a nice surprise it is too," he said with a smile.

She told him that once the baby came she would not have the time or energy to do it for a while, so she wanted to treat him to a special dinner. Rhodri was over the moon. They called the boys down for dinner. As they gathered around the table, their father told them that they would be lucky if they married a woman just like their mother. Geraint and Dai gave a groan. Girls were still yucky to the two of them and the very thought of marriage disgusting.

Morgan called out, "I'll marry you."

"Why Morgan, are you proposing to me?" his mother asked.

A look of puzzlement came over his face. "No Mama, I want to marry you."

"Ah boyo, that's nice, but I'm already married. What about your father?" she said reminding him.

Morgan asked his father if it was all right for him to marry her too.

Rhodri replied, with a smile, "Well boyo, I've always tried to teach you to share; I guess I'll have to learn to do it too."

Rhodri could tell that he was confused by his answer so he made it clear to him. "Sure boyo, it's all right with me."

Morgan jumped in his chair with excitement, "Yeah, I can marry Mommy!"

They all began to laugh, even Geraint and Dai thought it was funny. As soon as their meal was over Mari asked the boys to bring the tub up from the cellar. While they were retrieving the wash tub, she began heating water for their baths. While Morgan was taking his bath, and after Geraint and Dafydd had completed theirs, they joined their father in the sitting room. Mari would be some time in the kitchen helping Morgan bathe and cleaning up the dishes. When she came into the sitting room, she sat on the settee and worked on darning some socks while Morgan snuggled up close beside her. Rhodri was telling stories, as usual, and as usual, Geraint and Dafydd were thoroughly engrossed in them. The clock chimed ten. Mari glanced over at Rhodri and then back at Morgan who had fallen asleep with his head in her lap. He got the hint, finished his story and told the boys that it was way past their bedtime. They went without a fuss. Mari thought to herself that if she had told them that it was bedtime instead of Rhodri, they would have argued with her over it. Rhodri woke Morgan up and told him to go to bed.

"I wasn't sleeping; I was just resting my eyes," Morgan insisted, still half asleep, rubbing his eyes.

"It's late and it's time for bed. We're coming up too. Now scoot. You're getting too big to carry," his father told him.

When Rhodri and Mari went to bed shortly after they had sent the boys, they could hear noises. They thought that it was the boys goofing around at first and were heading towards their room to warn them to go to sleep when they realized that the noise was coming from next door. Sean was at it again. Rhodri was going to bang on the wall, but Mari stopped him.

"You'll only make things worse for Cate. Let's give 'im a minute. Maybe he'll stop?"

She was right. Within a few minutes everything died down. They were not sure if the fight was over, but they could no longer hear them. Rhodri fell asleep as soon as his head hit the pillow. Mari was having a hard time shutting off her mind and getting comfortable. She was worried about Cate, and no matter what position she tried, she just couldn't seem to drift off to sleep. She was awake practically all that night. When Rhodri woke in the morning, he nudged Mari. She could not believe that it was already time to get up. She heard the clock strike seven and knew he was right. She went downstairs to make breakfast. She complained to Rhodri about how tired she was. He decided that she should stay home from the game and take a nap. He said that Geraint and Dai could keep an eye on Morgan while he was playing. He knew that she would not be able to sleep if he left Morgan there with her, and besides that, Morgan liked going to the games too. When the boys came down, their father told them that Morgan would be coming with them, but not their mother.

"Your mother's tired today, so we are going to let her have the house all to herself," he said.

"Who's gonna watch Morgan?" questioned Geraint, fearing what the answer would be.

"Why you and Dai will. I've gotta play," he told them.

Mari looked over at Geraint and Dafydd. "You boys wouldn't mind looking after your little brother for a few hours, now would you?"

"Ah, do we have to?" they both moaned.

"Yes, you do," she replied sternly.

"OK boyos, you heard your mother. Let's go."

He gave Mari a kiss goodbye and instructed her to forget about the breakfast dishes; she needed her rest. She walked out onto the porch and watched them walk down the street. She intended to do just as Rhodri said. She figured she could always do the dishes after her nap.

"What a luxury just to be able to take a nap," she thought to herself.

She cleared her mind and laid down and fell fast asleep. She knew that she would not be disturbed for at least a couple of hours, maybe longer if she was lucky. Mari was confident that the boys would have a good time, and why wouldn't they? The baseball diamond was a beautiful place to spend the day. It was a perfect location and the best diamond that the mining teams played. Everyone in New Salem was proud of it, located on top of a hill at the other end of town, near the company housing. The men of the town had removed all the grass within the diamond itself, and made a proper pitcher's mound. Every place else was lush and green, and without a tree in or around the playing field. They had benches for the two teams and had even constructed a concession stand where there was always enough beer to go around. The townies that came would often pack a lunch and bring their blanket to make a day of it. It was the best entertainment in the area, and you couldn't ask for a more picturesque setting. From the diamond you could see the rolling hills leading into the Allegheny Mountains, showing off some little hamlets in the distance. Wild flowers dotted the countryside, and at that time of year, the mountain laurels were in full bloom. It was a spectacular sight to behold.

The crowd's exuberant cheers for a double play, a home run, or an out, carried down the hill all the way back to the company housing. Even those not attending the game could usually tell if the home team was winning or losing by the roars coming from the diamond. When Mari came to the games, she and the boys sat in a specific spot to watch the game. Normally the boys enjoyed watching the game, but not that day. They had more important things to do, like hunt down either Tommy or Orville or anyone else that knew what had started the fight the day before. Geraint spotted Mrs. Turner at the game with her two children and asked if she would not mind keeping an eye on Morgan.

He used the excuse that they had forgotten something back at their house. She told them that she did not mind helping them out, but to be quick about it. Geraint and Dai assured her that they would not be long, and they took off to see what they could find out. They looked, but Tommy was nowhere around. Finally, they saw Orville walking up the hill towards the diamond. Now Orville Jenkins was known to everyone as a great fabricator of stories. Tommy would have been more truthful about what had happened, but they were certainly guaranteed a better tale from Orville. What really happened was a mere detail to him. He could weave a lie into a labyrinth of fiction that would entertain you to the core. Orville stopped, sat on a tree stump and smoked a cigarette that he had stolen from his father. He knew he had little time before the game started. Geraint and Dafydd approached him as he slowly exhaled his first drag.

"I'd give you guys one but it's all I got," he told them.

They shrugged it off like "oh well", as neither of them smoked anyways.

Geraint never liked beating around the bush and got right to the point. "So what happened Friday?"

"What? With Tommy?" asked Orville.

"Yeah with Tommy. Who do you think?" Geraint said impatiently.

"We had a fight," was Orville's response as he shrugged his shoulders as though it was no big deal.

"Yeah, no kidding; we saw that much. Why were yah fighting?" Dafydd asked, dying to know what happened.

"Ah, he thought I did his sister wrong or something. No big deal. I'd have killed him if old man Langdon hadn't come sticking his nose in, busting it up," bragged Orville.

"Which sister?" the boys asked.

"Maureen," said Orville with a grin.

"Ooooh she's so ugly. What did yah do to her?" Geraint asked.

"Nah, we did it to each other," he hinted with a grin on his face.

"What did you guys do?" prompted Dafydd.

"What do yah think we did, stupid? The horizontal rumble tumble," Orville declared to the boys.

"Ooooh, how could you even kiss her with those teeth of hers?" whined Dafydd.

"Yeah, I know, they're something, all right. Her teeth are so bucked out she could eat corn through a fence. But let's just say, she could lick the butter off my cob anytime... if yah know what I mean," Orville bragged raising his eyebrows and elbowing them.

Geraint and Dai shuddered and groaned as the image of the likes of the two of them together raced into their minds.

"Don't tell me Tommy caught you guys doin' it?" groaned Geraint.

"Hell no. Come on, you know I'm slicker than that. I guess Maureen must have let it slip or something. Oh, she was probably crying her little eyes out about me poppin' her cherry… but yah know what the funny thing is; that's not what pissed him off," claimed Orville.

"You're kidding," inquired Dafydd.

"Na, he got pissed off over something I said, not what I did."

"And what was that?" they both asked.

"Well, when Tommy came around acting tough, like he was going to defend her honor or something, I just told him, 'Hey, you should be thanking me.' She sure as hell was, and for some reason, I think that's what pissed him off more than me doing her." He shrugged.

The boys were laughing about the whole thing when Dai remembered that they left Morgan with Mrs. Turner.

"Hey, we gotta get back. It don't take that long to run home," complained Geraint.

"See yah, we gotta go. Tell Maureen we said hello," the boys laughed as they left Orville sitting rubbing the cigarette butt into the bark of the stump before he too went and watched the game.

They went rushing back to check on the game. Mrs. Turner had not seemed to notice that they had been gone for a while. She did ask them what it was they forgot to get. Geraint blurted out the first thing that came to his mind.

"Our mother's not well today. We wanted to go check on her."

"Ah, what good boys you two are," replied Mrs. Turner.

They sat down and enjoyed the rest of the game, with Morgan, Mrs. Turner, and her children. By the time they had rejoined the game, their father's team was ahead by three runs.

Back at the house, Mari had just woken up from a lovely sleep. It was so quiet and peaceful, it seemed as though the whole town was at the game that day. She went downstairs to wash the breakfast dishes that were still on the table and stove. As soon as the dishes were finished she heard the clock strike ten.

"Ah, sounds like I have time for a cup of tea," she thought to herself.

Just as she was beginning to pump the water into the kettle, hers hit the floor.

"SHITE!"

She thought that she had felt a few contractions, but they were not strong enough to concern her. Now her tea would have to wait. She calmly went and retrieved the mop from the cellar to clean the mess she had just made on the floor. She carefully made her way down the narrow, dark stairs. The water was still leaking from her. She was mad at herself for not putting a towel between her legs before grabbing the mop. After getting the mop, she backed her way up the stairs, mopping each one as she went. A strong contraction grabbed hold of her as she reached the top step. She braced herself with the mop handle until the contraction was over.

"Ooh, now that was a strong one," she whispered to herself, trying her best to stay calm, as she finished mopping the water off the stairs and floor. Another contraction. They were coming faster and stronger. She had assumed, at the onset, that she had lots of time before she needed help. She now knew that her assumption was wrong. She was already feeling the need to push. She made her way over to Cate's front door, which was closed. She knocked, but there was no answer. She knocked louder. Still no answer. Another contraction. Now she was beginning to panic. She began beating on the door and calling for help. Still no answer. She was all alone and terrified. Another contraction, this one was so strong it dropped her to her knees. She tried to call out for help, but, because of the pain, all she could muster was a groan of agony. Tears were streaming down her face. Still on her knees another contraction grabbed her. After it ended, she tried to lift herself up by grasping a nearby chair. As she tried to make it to her feet she called out one more time. "Somebody, please help me!!" Just then Cate came running up onto the front porch.

"Sweet baby Jesus," said Cate as she made it to her friend. "Don't worry, I'll get you inside. Damn it, I went to the market. But I'm here now."

"Oh, thank God you got here. Cate, I was so scared."

"Ann, get the doctor... NOW!... Kelly, help me lift Mari so we can get her in the house."

Cate and Kelly tried to get under her shoulders to lift, but as they did Mari had another contraction and begged them to put her down.

"Leave me here," she cried. "It's too late. The baby's coming now!"

"Hold on, sweetie," said Cate as she too began to panic.

Cate instructed Kelly to go into the house and grab the linens and towels that Mari had set aside. When Kelly brought them out, she sent her back inside to heat a pot of water. As she was doing that, she heard her mom call out again.

"Get me a pillow."

Kelly grabbed one off the settee and took it out to her mom. Cate tried to position it under Mari's head, and told her to lean back on it.

"OK, sweetie, let's see what we've got," she said nervously.

Mari groaned with another contraction. By this time, an elderly couple from across the street heard the commotion and came out on their porch to investigate. They called over to see if they needed any help. "I need a doctor," she called out. "Where the hell is Ann with that doctor? Oh my God, Mari, don't push anymore. Your baby's breached!"

Cate wanted to turn the baby, but she was afraid it had come too far into the birth canal for that. All she could see was the baby's rear end. By this time, Mari was pleading. An image of what happened to Cate's aunt Beth came crashing into memory. She and her baby died during a breach childbirth. All Cate could think of was that she needed to get the baby out before the positioning of the baby killed the two of them.

"Come on, sweetie, you can do it. The worst is over. Now push... harder... harder. That's good, good. The baby's almost out now," Cate said wiping the sweat from her brow.

Mari was thrashing about in excruciating pain. Cate couldn't even imagine how she was holding on. She had ripped badly and was losing a lot of blood. Cate was horrified at the thought of losing her friend. Kelly dampened an end of a towel and wiped Mari's brow. Cate told Kelly to go inside and prepare the sofa. She wanted to get Mari inside as soon as she could. Mari was extremely weak now. She was moaning things that Cate did not understand.

"Mari, come on... Help me now, concentrate... just one more good push should do it. Come on, Mari, you can do it. Push," Cate encouraged.

Ann and the doctor came up just as Mari gave her last effort. Cate was so relieved that the doctor was there to take over. Dr. Pritchard, with the help of his forceps, delivered the baby. Mari was, by then, unconscious. Ann held the baby as the doctor and Cate tried to lift her into the house. When they moved her, the placenta fell out onto the porch. Ann and Kelly both screamed when they saw it, not knowing what it was. The doctor calmed them down, telling them that it was normal, and needed to come out. They took Mari inside and laid her down on the sofa. Dr. Pritchard stitched her up while she was still unconscious. He was concerned about the amount of blood that she had lost. Mari was white as a sheet and shivering uncontrollably as she drifted in and out of consciousness.

The doctor cleared his throat. "Her body has been through a great ordeal, and she has lost a lot of blood. The next twenty-four hours are critical. We have done all we can do. She is in God's hands now."

He checked the baby over. "She sure is a strong little girl. Her face is pretty bruised, but all in all, she's going to be fine."

Rhodri walked in the front door and asked, "What the hell is that shite on the porch?"

Cate hushed him and motioned for him to go outside. She met him on the porch while the doctor was packing up his instruments. She told Rhodri that Mari had a very difficult time, and that the next twenty-four hours were critical.

"Will she be all right?" he asked.

"She's lost a lot of blood," Cate informed him.

"I can see that," he said looking around the porch.

"You will have to leave her on the sofa for the night. She shouldn't be moved. She's very weak. The baby's bruised, but she's fine," Cate told him looking for some good news.

"It's a girl? Ah, Mari must be over the moon," Rhodri said relieved.

"Mari doesn't know yet. She fainted just as the baby was being born. You can tell her as soon as she regains consciousness. She will be very pleased about the news," Cate assured him. As she tried to console Rhodri, Sean came up on the porch and stood behind him and glared at Cate. The doctor came out and told Rhodri that there was nothing else that he could do, but that if he needed him he knew where he would be.

Rhodri asked the doctor if his wife would be all right.

He shook his head not knowing, but told Rhodri that he would call on them early in the morning. Cate could see the concern on his face and told him to go inside and check on his wife. She volunteered to clean up the mess on their front porch. As soon as Rhodri went inside she began apologizing to Sean, telling him that she was terrified and didn't know what to do.

His cruel response was, "Bullshit, you always know what to do for everyone except me. How long do you plan on staying over here?"

"Ah, I don't know. A little while," she answered impatiently to her husband.

Just then Rhodri came back outside. "Mari's sleeping, and the baby is getting fussy with Ann. Do you think she's hungry?"

"I don't know. She might be. I'll come check on her as soon as I'm done out here," she told him.

Rhodri went back inside to be with his wife. He wanted to be there when she opened her eyes.

"Yeah, why don't you go in and make sure the baby

gets fed. Don't worry about me," Sean snarled, turned his back and walked into their house, letting the screen door slam behind him. Kelly came out to help her mother.

Cate said, "Ah, thanks Kelly. You know what, forget helping me; go on home and get your father something to eat. I've got to go in and check on the baby as soon as I'm done here."

"Ma, you saw how he was. I don't want to go home. He'll just yell at me," Kelly protested.

"All right, just forget it. I guess he can manage." Cate gave her daughter a hug and told her, "I can't blame you. Believe me, I don't want to go home either."

Cate went in and took care of the baby, while checking on Mari. She told Rhodri that if he needed anything in the night to feel free to come and get her, knowing that if he did, Sean would pitch a fit. She gathered up the girls, telling them it was time to come home. Before they left, Rhodri asked Kelly if she could spend the night to help out with the boys.

Cate winked at Kelly. "I think that's a wonderful idea, don't you, Kelly?"

Kelly was so relieved that she didn't have to go home and face her father that she would have done just about anything.

"I'd love to stay and help," she insisted.

Ann was a little put out. She wanted to stay too, and Cate could not blame her for that. But, only one of them was needed for the job, and Mr. Evans only asked for Kelly simply because she was the oldest. Cate instructed Ann as soon as they were outside, "Go straight to your room and be quiet. Read something. I'll bring you up some food as soon as I can."

Ann knew the drill. Luckily for Ann, her father was out in the backyard drinking when they walked into the house. She was able to sneak up the stairs without having to speak to him, or he to her. Cate warned her that she knew as soon he was back in the house he was going to be nasty and, no matter what, she was to stay in her room. Sean could hear Cate stirring around in the kitchen. He came staggering in through the kitchen door drunk.

"I'm making you something to eat. It'll just be a few

minutes," Cate told him.

"I thought I told you, don't worry about me. I'm drinking a bottle for supper, just like the baby," he said sarcastically.

"Where's the girls? Why the hell aren't they in here helping you?" he scoffed.

"Ann's upstairs doing homework. Kelly's going to spend the night next door to help Rhodri with the kids. I didn't think it would be a problem," Cate said.

"That is the problem. You don't think, do yah? I swear you're as dumb as a lump of coal. If Rhodri needs help, everybody jumps. Where's my help? No wonder the girls are lazy. You let them do anything they want. Spoiled brats," he argued.

"How can you say that? They are not spoiled. They're good girls," she defended.

"Then you're not only stupid, you're blind too," he barked at her.

Cate tried her best to ignore him. She changed the subject while she fixed him some food.

"You should see the baby. She's going to be so pretty, once the bruising and swelling goes away. She looks just like Mari. God, I hope she is going to be all right. The doctor said the next twenty-four hours are critical. She was so weak and you..."

Sean interrupted her, "Would you shut the fuck up about the neighbors. Jesus Christ, why do you always choose them over me? I'm your husband. I should come first. Why can't you ever be on my side?"

"Sides, Sean? Let's not fight about sides. I am on your side. It's just..."

He interrupted again, this time standing toe to toe with her, pointing his finger within an inch of her face, yelling, "I'm sick of your excuses. I've had them up to here," he said lifting his hand as though he were saluting her, "and yah know what else I'm sick of YOU!"

He continued to ramble on about how she mistreated him. She just stood at the stove staring at the hot cast iron skillet. She considered picking up the pan and smacking him as hard as she could across his thick head. She had to dismiss the thought, knowing that he would overpower her and use it on her. She could not let him kill her even though many times she would have liked to have died, but for the girls' sake, she had to be strong and not allow herself to give into temptations. She could not imagine Sean raising the girls without her there. Cate did not feel that she could defend herself against his attacks because half of the time she did not understand why he was so angry. When they first got married, she took everything he said to her to heart. After a few years of his abuse, she was able to block out most of what he said to her during a fight. It was self-preservation. It was not something she had control over; it just happened. It started gradually.

They would have a huge fight and he would start name-calling as he always did. Afterwards she realized that there were small parts of the fight that she could not remember, even if she tried. When it first started to happen, it troubled her that she was having blackouts concerning the details of their fights. It did not take long before she embraced them as though they were a port in a storm, and in fact, for her they were. She found that entire events had been missing from her memory; she only wished that the girls could do the same. Being religious, in her way of thinking divorce just was not an option. She wished that he would die every day; it was a fantasy for her. She even knew how she wanted his headstone to read: "Here lies rotten Sean. We're happy now. He's dead and gone." She felt completely and utterly trapped. Many times, she would get up in the middle of the night not being able to sleep and go into the back yard to have a good cry. Her thinking had become clouded, and she had trouble remembering simple things. That is the problem with abuse. It is devastating as well as debilitating, and verbal abuse is often times worse than physical abuse. Words do not leave marks on the skin, only in the heart, mind and spirit. Sean rarely became violent, but the propensity towards violence was present and she felt violated by his irrational behavior. It was a fearful thing to be in his presence while he was angry. She never knew when he would turn physical. Once, in the middle of a huge fight, Sean blackened Catherine's eye with his fist. The first thought that came to her was that of relief instead of pain. She could finally see the abuse in the mirror instead of just feeling it inside.

She sat his meal on the table.

"Finally," he said.

He sat down at the table, bowed his head and prayed.

Cate and their girls about gagged every time he prayed. They could not understand why he bothered. They did not think his prayers went any higher than the ceiling. He barely got the "amen" out of his mouth when he started in on her again. She was relieved that Kelly was next door, and did not have to listen to his nonsense. Cate was exhausted after the trials of that day, and now the two nights of fighting with Sean. She was dead on her feet. She stood up and declared that as far as she was concerned the conversation was over and that she was going to bed. To her surprise, Sean did not say another word. She went up the stairs and collapsed on the bed, and fell into a deep sleep. She woke to a horrible nightmare. In her dream, a faceless man with a gun was chasing her and her girls. They were running as fast as they could, but they were in slow motion. They found a place to hide, but the faceless man found them. They ran into an alleyway, but there was no exit. She tried to protect the girls by standing in front of them, but when the man shot, the bullets went through her and killed Kelly and Ann. They all fell to the ground with Kelly and Ann's bodies lying on top of her. She knew that they were dead, and was terrified to move. She did not want the faceless man to shoot her again. She could feel the warm blood from Kelly and Ann flowing out of their bodies all over her. She could taste their blood in her mouth as she lay motionless, scared to breathe, waiting for the faceless man to leave. He stood over their bodies looking for a sign of life. She was afraid to move a muscle knowing he was still there.

She woke up with her heart racing. She rolled over telling herself that it was only another bad dream. She noticed that

Sean was not in the bed. Before her eyes could adjust to the light within the room, she thought, for a moment, the faceless man was standing at the foot of her bed. It was Sean; he was just standing there looking at her while she slept. It completely unnerved her. She asked him to come back to bed, which he did.

She had a hard time shaking off the nightmare and the fright that Sean had given her when she abruptly woke up. She did go back to sleep, but it was a very light sleep. She kept waking up to see if he was still in the bed. She had no idea what he was thinking about or how long he had been standing there staring at her while she was asleep. The only thing she could think of was that he was thinking about killing her. There was just no telling, and she was not going to ask him. She just wanted to make it through the night. She was still tired when she felt Sean stirring in the bed. She could have used a few more hours sleep, but she got up with him. She made him a cup of tea and started his breakfast. As she placed his breakfast in front of him, he gently put his arm around her waist and thanked her. She gave a deep sigh, knowing the fight was now over, at least for the time being. He was pleasant and calm as he sat at the kitchen table finishing his breakfast. Ann came down the stairs quietly and checked to see if her mother needed any help.

Her father greeted her with, "Good morning, sunshine."

"Good morning, Father," she responded.

"Come on and sit down. Your ma will have your breakfast lickety-split. You must be starving," he said thinking that she had nothing to eat the night before, which she had not.

Her mother had forgotten all about bringing her something to eat, so she was hungry. She took her father's directive and sat down, just as he was getting up. He told them that he was going out for a few hours and that he would see them later. He made the comment that he was sure that they were eager to go next door and check on Mari and the baby. He gave Cate a hug and a kiss before he left. When he stepped outside, he saw Dafydd and Geraint playing a game of marbles in the front yard. He stopped and talked to them for a minute. He remarked how nice it would be for them to have a baby sister, and that they would be great big brothers.

As soon as Cate cleaned up the kitchen and got dressed, they went next door to see Mari and her new baby. Sean was right; they were eager to go. She had no idea where Sean had gone, and did not care. On a Sunday, the bars did not open. Cate told Ann not to say anything about the fight that had taken place the night before. She hoped that they did not hear anything through the walls. When they got there, no one said a word about the fight. Cate was relieved.

Mari was still pale and weak, but at least she was alive. Kelly told her mother that Dr. Pritchard had already been by to examine Mari's condition and said that she would be fine, but that she needed complete bed rest for a few days.

Mari told Cate, "I'm so sore I couldn't get up if I wanted to, and having Kelly here was a godsend."

"I'm sure Kelly enjoyed every minute," Cate told Mari.

Kelly asked her mother if it was all right if she volunteered to stay with Mari until she was stronger. Cate told her that it was all right with her, but that she would have to ask her father.

Mari said, "Oh that would be wonderful if she could stay over. It is so nice to be waited upon hand and foot. I feel just like the Queen of Sheba."

"Yes, I think that would be a wonderful idea, and I don't see how Sean could object to it." Actually she thought he probably would be angry about it, but at the moment, she couldn't care less as to what he thought.

Cate leaned over the cradle to peek at the baby. There were still some bruises, but the swelling had gone down. She was all bundled up as tight as a bug in a rug.

"I'll make us some tea and toast," Cate said getting to her feet.

"That sounds lovely," thanked Mari.

The baby started to fuss as they were having their tea. Kelly moved to the cradle to pick her up when Ann protested.

"It's my turn. You've had her all night."

"Girls, do not fight. Everyone will get her turn, and right now it's my turn," Cate insisted, picking the baby up.

"Hush now, don't you cry. Ah Mari, what a little darling. Have you picked out a name yet?" Cate asked, holding her tight.

Mari was pleased to tell her that she and Rhodri decided on a name.

"She'll be called Catherine Gladys after you and my mother."

Cate was thrilled, but started to blush and chuckle when she heard the name.

Mari asked her what she thought was so funny.

Cate's face became redder. "When you said her middle name was going to be Gladys, all I could think of was how glad I was to see her ass out of there. Not that Gladys is a funny name."

Mari chuckled and said, "I hadn't thought of that. I guess, under the circumstances, it is kind of funny since she came out butt first."

Kelly and Ann were embarrassed by what their mother said, but they did think it was funny. Cate cradled Catherine in her arms, glowing with pride. She never had anyone name a baby after her before.

"Catherine Gladys Evans. What a beautiful name for a beautiful little girl," Cate boasted.

She was a beautiful baby. As soon as she opened her eyes, Cate thought that she was a little angel. The color of her eyes was a deep azure, and she had the longest lashes Cate had ever seen. Her lips were the color of pink rose petals, and she had the cutest button nose. Her hair was dark and already had some curl to it. Cate could not get over how different she looked from the day before. She was gorgeous.

Morgan came into the sitting room and sat on the settee next to Ann. He had wetted his hair and combed it straight back, and had gotten into his father's cologne. The girls could smell him coming before he entered the room. He thought he looked so handsome. He was obviously smitten. About that time, Sean came to the door. He knocked before he came into the Evans house.

"I guess I know where my family is," he said.

As soon as Sean came in, Kelly asked if she could stay there for a few days to help. She was hoping that he would not say no in front of Mari. She was right. He told Kelly that he did not mind and that it was kind of her to offer. He joked with Mari, telling her that when they got their grocery bill they would be sorry they kept her. Kelly rolled her eyes, embarrassed that he talked about her appetite like that. He liked to make comments in front of people about how much she ate and how big he thought she was. Because of that, she would not eat much in front of him. She could not count the times she left the table in tears because of the names he would call her. She began eating in secret, hiding food in her room. Cate knew she did it, but ignored it.

Cate changed the subject. "Guess what they named her?"

"How the hell would I know what they called her," he paused for a second and replied, "Jezabel, after you?" unwittingly revealing his dark side." "I wouldn't have a clue," Sean said.

"You got that right," Cate thought, then said, "Catherine Gladys, after me and the baby's grandma who died back in Wales."

Mari made mention that the baby was hungry and needed to be fed. Sean did not want to witness that and decided that it was time for him to leave. Cate told him that she would be there in a minute. Rhodri came in as Sean was leaving.

"She sure is a looker," Sean commented.

"Yeah, Mari's a beauty all right," Rhodri told him.

Sean laughed. "I meant the baby."

Ann and Cate left, leaving Kelly there tending to Mari's needs. Rhodri asked Mari if she was hungry. She told him that she should eat something.

"I'll go fix all of us a little something."   "You're a fine husband, and I'm lucky to have you,"
she said lovingly.

"I can't argue with that."

He went into the kitchen and cut some sandwiches for him and the boys, and brought his wife a bowl of soup. Rhodri made sure that his wife had all of the assistance she needed until she regained her strength. Cate came over every day while the men were working during Mari's recuperation.

four

THE GAME

Three years had come and gone since Catherine's birth. The big news now was coming out of Europe. In July 1914, Austria issued a declaration of war against Serbia. Within a few days of that event other countries followed and were joining in the conflict: Germany, Hungary, Turkey, Bulgaria, France, Russia, Japan, the Brits, not to mention Portugal, Italy, and even Liberia. It seemed like the whole world had gone mad. Combatant armies were all over Europe and beyond. The western front was a continuous line of trenches that extended from the Belgian coast, through France, to the Swiss border. Reports coming out of Europe were surreal. Americans especially disturbed by the reports, were those that had lived through the Civil War some fifty years earlier. Dread filled their hearts with the mere prospect of Northerners and the Southerners having to join together, arm-in-arm, to fight against a common enemy in a foreign land. The ghastly scenes from the Civil War still haunted them. They were transfixed with terror, and told horrific stories about the losses they had endured. They spoke of battles as though they had only happened yesterday.

Local men, Ned Owens and Samuel Hunter, were both survivors of the battle of Gettysburg. In fact, just a year earlier, the two men made a pilgrimage to the old battlefield. They took part in a fiftieth anniversary reunion sponsored by the federal government. The reunion lasted three days, just like the original conflict. They were joined by thousands of survivors bivouacked on the grounds of the battlefield in Gettysburg. Some of the men went to look up old comrades, while some were drawn to revisit the spot where their friends and fellow soldiers had fallen. All those in attendance had incredible stories of bravery to swap. It was a sobering affair.

The highlight of the event for many of the veterans, North and South, was the re-enactment of Pickett's Charge. The visiting Union veterans went to Cemetery Ridge and took their position behind a small stone wall, just as they had on that fateful day fifty years earlier. They watched and waited for their former adversaries to emerge from their place in woods along Seminary Ridge. Their hearts raced at the first glimpse of the Confederate veterans coming into view from amongst the line of trees and into the open field. Closer and closer they came, a bit slower pace this time. Instead of guns and bayonets glistening in the sunshine, their crutches and canes came close to yielding the same effect. As the Southerners approached the Northerners' position, they attempted to do their famous rebel yell. It wasn't the same. The last time that the Northerners heard the likes of it, their hearts filled with fear. This time, it moved them with compassion.

They climbed over the wall and ran into the field embracing their former foes. They fell upon each other's necks and wept over the senseless loss each side had endured. Because of their trial by fire, they now had mutual respect one for the other. The reckoning was done, but the repugnance of the battle would always remain in their hearts. It was still hard for the men to believe that in just three days, the longest three days these men had ever lived through, fifty-one thousand of their friends and fellow soldiers fell on the Gettysburg battlefields. They shared stories about their battles, from the Devil's Den, to the Round Tops, to the Wheat Fields, to the Valley of Death. The awful sights and sounds of the struggle, a half a century later, still echoed in their hearts and minds. It was described as three days of hell on earth, and that was just one battle. The Civil War lasted four years, and in that span of time, six hundred thousand men and boys were lost. The thought of war for the survivors wasn't an adventure as many of them first thought it to be. It was a nightmare that they hoped would never be repeated. The reunion at Gettysburg was held every Memorial Day there after. Ned and Samuel felt compelled to make sure that no one in New Salem forgot what war was really all about.

Sam Watkins, a Confederate soldier, wrote his experiences of the Civil War as quoted, "Were these things real? Did I see those brave and noble countrymen of mine laid low in death and weltering in their blood? Did I see the ruins of smoldering cities and deserted homes? Did I see the flag of my country, that I followed so long, furled to be no more unfurled forever? Surely they are but the vagaries of mine own imagination... .But, hush! I now hear the approach of battle. That low, rumbling sound in the west is the roar of cannon in the distance." Sam Watkins was a soldier in Company H, First Tennessee Regiment.

Each day Rhodri searched the paper for news about the war in Europe, and each day it seemed to be worsening. Rhodri would give Mari a condensed version while she was busily doing her morning chores. He knew she did not have the luxury of time to peruse the paper, and besides that, they savored the time together without being accosted by their children. School was in recess for the summer, so there was no reason they could not spend some time alone early in the morning.

"Thank God for President Wilson. It says here that he's gonna stay out of the war and remain neutral. We sure don't want our boys going. I mean, why the hell would we send 'em there to get six bells of shit kicked out of 'em?" Rhodri commented.

Mari sighed shaking her head in agreement. "I am so glad our boys are young."

"Geraint's almost old enough, but I will tell you what, as long as President Wilson sticks to his guns, he will have my vote for a second term in office," assured Rhodri.

He gave her a kiss and picked up his lunch pail and canteen and left for work. While the children were still sleeping, she finished a few chores. It was about forty-five minutes before she heard them stirring. She knew it would not be long before they would all be down wanting their breakfast. Sure enough, within a few minutes, they began trickling down the stairs into the kitchen. Morgan was the first down, followed closely by little Catherine. It was ten minutes or so before Geraint and Dai were seen. Mari was busy making toast for them and had not noticed that the older boys had remembered to bring down the dirty clothes.

"Where do you want 'em?" Geraint asked.

She turned around and looked saying, "There in the corner will be fine. That was thoughtful of you."

"We made our beds too," bragged Dafydd.

She knew they had to be after something. "The beds too. And what would it be that you're after?" she asked.

"Can we go over to the baseball diamond and play? All the guys are gonna be there," Geraint said.

"Please, please, with sugar on top," Dai piped in.

"Yeah Ma, can we?" echoed Morgan.

Geraint glared at Morgan. "Hey, who invited you?"

"Hey yourself, boyo. I didn't say anyone could go, now did I?" Mari told Geraint in a scolding tone.

"Ah come on, Ma. Everyone's gonna be there," pleaded Dai.

"Well it seems to me, if everyone's gonna be there, Morgan can certainly go too. It's either everyone or no one, your choice," she argued in Morgan's defense.

A look of horror washed over Dafydd's face when he heard his mother say "everyone or no one". "Do we have to take Catherine too?" he asked.

"Of course not. She'll stay with me; I only meant Morgan," she explained.

"Oh all right, yah big baby, you can come too," snarled Geraint, not liking it one bit.

"Just for that, you can stay home and help me with laundry. Dai and Morgan can go without you," his mother told him.

Geraint knew that he had better apologize and fast.

"All right, I'm sorry, Morgan. You're not a big baby. In fact, you're a better player than Stanley Hayward ever was,"

Geraint said humbly.

"All right then. Finish your breakfast and off yah go," she told them.

"Thanks Ma," Geraint said relieved. He knew he had dodged a bullet that time.

They looked as though they were in a race to finish. They began wolfing down their food like there was no tomorrow. They bolted up the stairs as soon as they finished their last bite, grabbed their bat and mitts, and ran out the door. They were really looking forward to playing. It was not every day they could get enough kids together to have a proper game. They usually had to play a game called outs, where there was one batter and at least three fielders. First one to catch three balls would win the honor of being the next one at bat. It was a fun game, but not the same as a real game with all the players involved.

They ran into Orville as they reached the path that led up the hill to the diamond. He was sitting on a stump smoking. When he saw Geraint and Dai he offered them his last cigarette that he had balanced on top of his ear.

"You guys can share it if you wanna," Orville said handing them the cigarette.

Orville always had cigarettes that he stole off his old man while he was drunk. He claimed he was always too drunk to keep track of how many he had left. Geraint and Dai started to reach for it when they realized that Morgan was there and would tell on them if they smoked it.

Orville egged them on saying, "Ah, go on. The little asswipe wouldn't dare tell, would yah?" he said looking right at Morgan as he slashed at his throat with his hand in a threatening manner.

Morgan shook his head no. He was intimidated by Orville and did not want to get on his bad side.

"Better not, if yah know what's good for yah," he said continuing the threat.

Geraint and Dai shared the cigarette, both acting as though they inhaled. They offered Morgan a hit, but he declined

They waited for the rest of the boys to show up.

"Hey, did you guys hear what happened to old man Gilley?" Orville said starting to laugh.

"Was that you?" Geraint asked.

Neither Dafydd or Morgan knew what he was talking about.

"Why, what happened to Mr. Gilley?" asked Morgan.

"Ah my friends, I wish yah could have been there to see it. I haven't laughed so hard since my auntie got her tit caught in the mangle. Hey, it was better than what I pulled on old man Jones. Now I know yah heard 'bout that one, right?" he asked thinking his antics were legendary.

Orville could tell by the looks on their faces, that they hadn't.

Orville rolled his eyes. "Damn, what the hell do yah guys do, walk around with your head up your ass?"

Geraint started laughing and elbowed Dai. "You do too know 'bout Mr. Jones, the bag of crap."

"Oh that," Dafydd said, but Morgan still didn't know what they were talking about, which was fine with Orville since he was dying to repeat it.

"Hey, yah oughta try this one; it's funny as hell. First I filled a bag with some dog shit and put it by his front door. Then, you're gonna love this, I set it on fire knocked his door and ran. You should have seen his face when he stomped on the bag to put the fire out. There was shit everywhere; I really filled that bag up. God, that was funny," Orville explained with glee.

Morgan stood there in awe of what he was hearing. He would never try anything like that. Morgan could not fathom the prank that Orville must have pulled on poor Mr. Gilley.

Both Dai and Morgan were wide eyed as they questioned what he had done this time.

"Ah it was the best. My old man left half a bottle of gin when he passed out the other night so I helped myself, knowing he'd never miss it. Anyhow, I was walking around getting shit-faced when, lo and behold, I spotted old man Gilley going into his outhouse. I knew he didn't see me so I ran up and pushed on the door to block him inside. Well I guess I didn't know my own strength cuz the whole damn thing started to tip, so I pushed harder. You should have heard him screaming. He was going nuts in there. I pushed the whole damn thing over with him in-side. If he ever found out it was me, he'da killed me. You should have seen him when he crawled out. He looked like a giant turd. It was great. I laughed so hard I pissed myself." Orville nearly pissed himself again simply repeating the story.

The only reason Geraint knew anything about it at all was he overheard his parents talking. He had only gotten part of their conversation when they shooed him out of the room, but he had heard enough for him to suspect that Orville was behind it. The boys were sworn to secrecy. More of the boys had shown up by then so they made their way up the hill to the diamond. It was a warm sunny day, not a cloud in the sky. They gathered in front of the concession stand to choose sides. Orville, of course, appointed himself captain of the one team. Tommy was captain of the other. Orville tossed the bat to Tommy. He caught it about half way down the shaft. Back and forth they placed their hands on top of each other until they came close to the top. Orville, in a brilliant move, cupped his hand over the top so his fingertips touched Tommy's hand and called out, "Eagle claws. I get first pick and we get first ups."

All the boys lined up to be chosen by the two captains. As they were called, they moved out of the line and stood behind their captain. Orville's first pick was Geraint. Tommy had the next pick.

"Harry," Tommy called.

Dafydd was Orville's second choice.

Tommy then chose Ashley, followed by Carl and so on. Morgan and Stanley were the last ones picked so Morgan was on Tommy's team and Stanley ended up playing for Orville's side. The captains then took their players aside to assign them their positions. Not everyone had mitts, so they had to share with the other team. As the boys came in from the field for their team's turn at bat, they would toss their mitts in the dirt at the feet of the boy they were sharing with. By the second inning of the game, the gloves would be all sweaty and gritty with dust, but no one seemed to mind. It was a close game. Orville's team was down by two runs going into the ninth inning, but they were at bat. Watching the boys play was like watching a comedy of errors. Infield home runs were commonplace. Both teams were equally bad, but they did, however, muster up some good plays now and then. Between plays there was a lot of nose picking, ball scratching, daydreaming, and spitting.

Stanley was on deck. As he approached the plate, he spit into his hands and took a few practice swings. Before Tommy threw his first pitch to Stanley, he scanned the field to see if his team was ready. They were as ready as they were going to be. They didn't have an umpire so they depended on the catcher to stay neutral and make the right calls. Their captain stood in back of him and watched, keeping him honest. The first pitch of the ninth was thrown. Stanley swung and missed.

"Strike one."

Stanley retook his batting stance. He felt confident that he would hit the next pitch. When the ball came across the plate, Stanley swung so hard he spun in a circle and almost dropped to his knees.

"Strike two," was the call.

Now he was getting nervous. The team was counting on him to get on base. He swung at the next pitch, tipping it foul into the air. Jimmy caught it and declared him out. Stanley would not even look in Orville's direction, but he could feel his glare on his back. He put down his bat and walked to the bench, kicking at the dirt, feeling disgraced. He heard Orville mumble, "Yah big girl's blouse," as he walked by, but at least he was quiet about it. He was hoping no one else heard him.

Marcus was up next. He picked up the bat that Stanley just used and warmed up a few feet from home plate as though he was going to cream the next ball. He had an awkward batting stance. He was a tall, thin boy and stood farther away from the plate than anyone else. As soon as the ball was pitched, he jumped in front of the plate and successfully bunted the ball and made it to first base. Tommy was caught off guard. He did not expect him to bunt. Geraint was up. Orville gave him a pat on the back and told him, "Go get 'im."

Tommy's pitch was low and outside. Geraint nailed it, popping it high into the air. Geraint took off like a bolt of lightning. Ashley rushed in to catch the ball. Orville's team was yelling for him to miss the catch. He came close to getting it, but he fumbled. Because of the near catch, Geraint only made it to first base; Marcus stopped at second. The next up to bat was Dafydd. Orville wanted Dafydd to try another bunt, but Dafydd did not think that he could pull it off as well as Marcus. When the ball was pitched, it was perfect for a grounder. Dafydd went for it. Unfortunately, he hit the ball straight towards the third baseman, sacrificing Marcus who was nearly there. Dafydd was only able to make it to first base. With two outs, two on base, and still two runs down, John was up. Tommy looked around the field at his team and decided that he needed to take control of this one. John was not much in the field, but behind the bat, if he ever got a hold of a decent pitch, he could easily hit a home run. Tommy was not about to let that happen. His first pitch was a fast one, straight at John's head. He instinctively jumped out of the way, but the ball clipped him in the shoulder forcing the walk to first base. The bases were loaded and Orville was mad as hell. He knew Tommy did that on purpose. Orville wanted revenge for the cheap shot aimed at John, and it was finally his turn at bat. He planned on hitting a line drive straight down Tommy's throat. His first pitch was way outside.

"Ball one," was called.

The second pitch was high.

"Ball two."

Orville really wanted a chance to hit the ball and be a hero, but it looked like Tommy had other plans, and was going to walk him, forcing one run. That would have left them one run short of a tied game and Tommy's team still had last bats.

The next pitch was inside. Orville took that as a warning that Tommy could hit him with the ball just like he had previously done to John. If looks could kill, Tommy would have dropped dead right where he stood.

"Ball three."

The next pitch was outside, but Orville leaned into it a caught enough of it for a grounder. Hank bent down to pick it up, but it went through his legs. By the time Tommy's team had regained control of the ball, Dafydd and Geraint scored two runs tying the game. John rushed to third base while Orville was safe on second. Billy was now at bat. The entire day had gone well for him, and he attributed his success to his brand new Louisville Slugger baseball bat that his father had just bought for him. It was his pride and joy. That bat made him feel as though he was invincible. Tommy pitched a fast ball and Billy creamed it, driving it deep into right field. John and Orville crossed home plate, making them ahead by two runs and Billy was coming rounding third. Orville's team was on their feet yelling, "Slide, Slide!"

He did, but the ball beat him home and he was called out at home plate. Orville's team now had a two-run lead. Tommy's team came in from the fields to take their last bats.

Orville had his team huddle around him for a pep talk before they took their positions in the fields.

"OK boys, let's get the sons-a-bitches. Three up and three down."

His team was chanting the phrase as they moved to their places, "Three up, three down; three up, three down."

Orville had also instructed his team that when they got to the bottom of the ninth to shout out "SWING" at every pitch. Orville's pitching was exceptional. He was as determined as he was focused.

Tommy stood behind Geraint, who was the catcher, to make sure his calls were fair. Carl approached the plate. He swung and missed the three pitches that came past him straight into Geraint's mitt. Orville's team heard Geraint call out the phrase that was music to their ears, "Strike three, you're out."

Harry came to the plate. He stood with his bat on the ground, the haft resting on his leg. He ran his fingers through his hair and adjusted his cap. He then spit on his hands before picking his bat up. He spread his legs shoulder width and slowly took his batting stance. He took two practice swings and nodded to Orville, acknowledging that he was now ready. His strategy was that if he could slow the play down a little, he would have a better chance of hitting the ball. Orville took a quick look around at his players while he tossed the ball into his own mitt. He then went into his wind up. His first pitch to Harry would have been a ball, but when he heard the team call out "SWING," he unwittingly obliged, and swung.

Orville announced to his team, "We have a live one, boys."

By now Harry was sweating. He knew they were going to do it again. Harry swallowed and tried his best to block the first strike out of his mind. He just wanted to focus on the next pitch, but every time he heard, "Hey batter, batter, swing," he swung wildly. He was an easy out. They only needed one more out to finish the game. Geraint started the chant again.

"Three up, three down."

The infield joined in the enthusiasm.

The next batter up was Tommy. Orville wanted to strike him out so bad, he could taste it. Tommy wanted Orville to taste something too, but he was thinking more in the lines of a line drive down his throat. That would teach him not to take advantage of his sister. Orville felt he had a score to settle because of Tommy hitting John with the pitch making him take the walk. He anxiously pawed the ground with the toe of his shoe. He rolled his shoulders and started his wind up. Tommy swung, missing the ball. He thought it was perfect for a line drive but it curved outside right into Geraint's glove.

"Strike one," Geraint called out.

The second pitch was straight as could be. Tommy got a piece of it, but tipped it foul behind him. Geraint immediately jumped into action like a gazelle. He caught the ball and won the game for his team. Just like that the game was over and Tommy was out. The exuberance of the team could not be quelled. They ran towards the pitching mound as though they had just won the World Series.

Orville called out to Tommy as he was leaving, "Ah, don't cry. Have your mammy wipe your ass."

"Hey, screw you. At least my mom's not a drunk like yours. She probably can't wipe her own ass," Tommy called out.

Normally, Orville would have gone after anyone who dared say anything about his family, but he let the comment pass, and just said, "Ah, sour grapes."

Geraint knew Orville hated anyone talking bad about his mother, even though she was a drunk. He got Orville's mind off it by quickly changing the subject. He compared Orville's pitching to Rube Waddell, the best pitcher the Philadelphia Athletics ever had.

Orville smiled and said, "Yeah, my pitching arm got so hot, I should have poured ice water on it just like Rube used to do before a big game."

Geraint's response to that was, "Yeah, my glove was smoking from the heat you were throwing."

Orville started doing cartwheels across the pitcher's mound. The boys laughed about it.

George Edward "Rube" Waddell had some queer mannerisms when he played the game, but no one could deny his abilities as a pitcher. He was born in Punxsutawney, Pennsylvania, and was the son of a farmer. His fast ball and his curve ball were legendary. His heavy drinking was also legendary. Sports writers labeled him "The Sousepaw." He claimed that he could not remember how many times he had married. When he was pitching he had a hard time concentrating on the game, and was easily distracted. Everything caught his eye. It did not matter if it was a pretty woman, a puppy, or even a shiny object; he could not help looking at it. He would even try to leave the field in the middle of a game if a fire truck went by. On some occasions his teammates would have to physically restrain him until the urge passed. When the season was over he sometimes wrestled alligators for a living.

Geraint asked Orville, "Remember the time he out-pitched Cy Young in the World Series?"

"Remember, hell, who could forget it? The damn game lasted twenty innings, for Christ's sake," Orville reminded him.

"Yeah, I wish I could have been there," said John.

Orville claimed, "Yeah, well, don't we all."

Geraint said, "Hey, you guys should come over and see my dad's scrapbook. He's got everything in it."

Dafydd added, "Yeah it's great. You wouldn't believe the clippings he's got."

Morgan, who by then had joined his brothers, added, "Really you should come over."

"Well look who's here," Orville said patting him on the back. "Hey, yah didn't play half bad, for a little ass-wipe that is. I might even pick yah next time. Then you'll know what it's like to be on a winning team for a change."

"Ha, Ha," Morgan responded, knowing that it was really high praise coming from Orville.

Geraint said, "Yeah, come on over. My dad loves to show off the pictures of his old rugby teams. He brought 'em with him all the way from Wales."

"Wales, who the hell's your dad, Noah?" Orville asked joking around.

"Yeah, yeah… I think you mean Jonah… nah, come on over," Geraint encouraged.

Orville was the only one that wanted to go. Nobody had ever invited him to their house before. The rest of the boys decided that they had better get home before they got into trouble. They all declined the invitation, except Orville.

"Do yah really think he'd let me look at it?" Orville questioned.

"Sure he will. He loves showing it off. But I do have to warn you about one thing," Geraint told Orville.

"What's that?" he asked.

"Yah better bring a spare ear cuz he'll talk the one you got off," Geraint said laughing.

Dafydd and Morgan both shook their heads, confirming that their dad did like to talk about sports. Orville was relieved and laughed with them. He thought for sure they were going to tell him that it would be best if he did not come over after all.

"Ah, I don't know, maybe you better ask first. If he says it's okay then I'll come over," Orville said nervously.

The Jenkins family had a bad reputation throughout the town. You did not have to go inside their home to know that it was filthy. Some homes are just like that. Anyone passing by could tell by the tattered filthy curtains hanging in the windows and the empty gin bottles strewn about the yard, that Mrs. Jenkins was not much of a housekeeper. Orville was the youngest of eleven children. Their oldest boy, Fred, had committed suicide a few years earlier. No one in the town knew exactly why he did it, only that it was bizarre. The rumors spread through the town like a wildfire fueled by the wagging tongues fanning the flames. It burned out of control and could not be quenched. It was sad really; Fred Jenkins was probably the most likeable member of their family. He broke into the local theater late one night and hung himself, which was strange in itself, but, what was really odd, is he was wearing a woman's fur coat when he was found dead hanging near the stage. It was all a mystery. Why the theater? As far as anyone knew, Fred had no known affiliation. No one could figure out how he obtained an expensive lady's fur coat when he and his family were the poorest family in New Salem. Whose coat was it, and why was he wearing it when he killed himself? No one knew the answers, but everyone had an opinion and ventured to guess.

One of the Jenkins girls ran away from home when she was fifteen and it was rumored that she became a prostitute up in Pittsburgh. Another one of the girls, Rosemary, left home when she was only thirteen. Mrs. Jenkins insisted that they had sent her to help a sick aunt in Michigan. No one believed it.

Everyone surmised that she had a bun in the oven, and rumor had it that Mr. Jenkins was probably the father of Rosemary's baby. There seemed to be an incestuous relationship between the two of them. Rosemary was the only child of the eleven that Mr. Jenkins doted over. She was known for sitting upon her father's lap well after the time acceptable. They walked around holding hands and whispering to each other. It made the townies uneasy when they were seen together. It was a queer relationship. She was putting on weight in her face and tummy when she was sent to live with her aunt in Michigan. Mrs. Jenkins was never the same after Rosemary was sent away. She and her husband were constantly at odds. She began drinking heavily, and had become as much of a drunk as her husband. He had been a drunk for as long as anyone in town could remember.

It didn't matter if it was only midday. If you saw her she would be staggering, if she could walk at all. She was so emaciated she appeared to be a walking skeleton. All of her clothes seemed at least three sizes too big. She dragged her feet because her shoes were too large. Everything was too large for her small frame. Even the purse she carried seemed too big and heavy for her frail little arms. She rarely left the house after Rosemary had gone, but when she did, you could spot her a mile away. She always wore too much makeup. Her pale complexion was accented by her ruby red lipstick and heavy rouge that was rubbed onto her wrinkled face. Her eyebrows were drawn on by pencil in the shape of narrow high hills. Her long gray hair was pin curled in the front and left long and scraggily in the back. Young Catherine was afraid of her. Whenever she saw her approaching, she hid behind Mari's skirt. Ethel assumed that Catherine was just shy and made a fuss over her every time she saw her. Ethel's speech would slur as she commented on how beautiful Catherine was and that she reminded her of Rosemary when she was that age. Mari tried to avoid her. The one time Ethel bent over and tried to compliment Catherine as to how pretty she was, Catherine mumbled, "Ooh, you uggee ceeeep." Fortunately, Ethel was drunk and did not understand her baby talk. Mari was embarrassd because she knew exactly what Catherine was trying to say. When she went home she told Rhodri about the incident between Catherine and Ethel Jenkins. He thought it was hysterical.

When Orville was seven years old, he was stabbed in the forearm with a fork by his father who happened to be fighting with his older brother, Bill. Orville bore the scar as a reminder of the last time he laid eyes on his brother and closest friend. He wrote to Orville a few times, but his father burned the letters unopened before he could retrieve them. From what little information Orville could gather, Bill had moved somewhere in Detroit, Michigan and worked in the Steel Industry. Orville believed the factory's name was Great Lakes Steel. One by one the Jenkins family fractioned off until Orville was the last of the children still living at home.

When the boys came home after the game, Geraint went inside to ask if they could have a friend over for supper. Dafydd and Morgan stayed outside with Orville while Geraint gained permission from their parents. Mari told him that she thought it would be all right, but that he needed to ask his father, who was out in the back-yard. Geraint told his father that a friend of his wanted to see the scrapbook and asked if he could eat with them too. He told him that his mother had already given permission but that he also needed his permission, which he gave. Geraint ran through the kitchen, thanking his mother as he went by for letting Orville stay for supper. She could hear Geraint telling Orville, who was standing on her front porch by then, that he was invited.

She stood at the stove in disbelief.

"Orville, did he say Orville?" she said raising her hand to her throat.

She went to the back door and asked Rhodri if he knew that he gave permission for a Jenkins to eat with them at the table.

"Nah, to tell the truth, I thought he was talking about Homer," Rhodri said scratching his head.

"Well he wasn't. He was talking about Orville. I

overheard him inviting him right on our front porch. Duw, I hope nobody saw that. You've got to go tell him it was a mistake," Mari said.

"Mari, come on now, we can't do that. We should have asked who he was inviting, but neither of us did, so that's our own fault. He can stay and eat and after he can look at the scrapbook just like I promised, and we will be kind to him, now won't we," Rhodri warned her with soft voice. He knew full well how upset his wife was about Orville coming to dinner and he did not want to antagonize her further.

Mari was as angry with herself as she was with her husband. She knew he would make her keep her word and allow him over for the evening, but she was furious with Geraint for not letting her know exactly who he had invited to their house. She thought he tricked her into letting someone into their house that she would never, in a million years, have allowed in, let alone feed and entertain.

Mari took a deep breath. "I am going to kill Geraint for this when it's over."

Rhodri patted her on the back to calm her down. "My luv, I think you just learned a valuable lesson, or should I say we both did."

"I'm still gonna kill 'im!" she threatened.

Mari walked back into the kitchen to finish their dinner as fast as she could. She wanted nothing more but to get Orville in and out of their home.

"Why cut the dog's tail off an inch at a time?" she thought to herself. She wanted Geraint to get Orville Jenkins off her front porch where everyone could see him. Mari was embarrassed by the thought of the neighbors knowing her son considered him a close enough friend to be invited over for a meal. Geraint came back through the kitchen a second time to ask his mother if his father was still in the back yard. She glared at him and pointed at the back door and ordered him to take Orville with him. Geraint could tell by her tone that she was mad about something, but shrugged it off as though it was no concern of his. He went back to the front and asked Orville to come in. By now, Orville was re-thinking the whole thing. He had never been invited to anyone's home before and he was getting very nervous about it. His palms were sweating at the thought of saying something wrong and possibly upsetting Geraint's parents. He didn't relish the thought of being tossed out on his ear, which is what he thought would happen, if he screwed up at the dinner table. He had been chased off by so many adults he thought it was strange for an adult to al-low him into his home. His stomach was beginning to flip think-ing about it. He decided that it would probably be best if he just went home.

Orville's voice began to crack as he told Geraint, "Yah know what? It's getting late; I should just go home," he said try-ing to excuse himself from what he was afraid would be an em-barrassing situation.

"Ah, come on, yah can't go now. Don't yah wanna see the scrapbook?" Geraint said, practically begging his friend to change his mind.

He really did want to see it, so he asked Geraint one more time.

"Are yah sure? I don't think your Ma and Dad are too keen on this," Orville said concerned.

"Nah, they're fine. My Ma's the one that told me to hurry up and get you inside. And besides, it's not like your Ma and Dad care if you come home or not," Geraint said, not thinking about the way it would sound to Orville.

Geraint was right and Orville knew it. His Mom and Dad wouldn't have known if he were around or not. Orville was at a loss for words. Their father called the boys in for dinner. Orville shrugged his shoulders not knowing what to do. He sheepishly walked across the threshold directly behind Geraint and stopped tugging on the back of Geraint's shirt not wanting to take anoth-er step inside. He had never felt so nervous in all his life. Dai and Morgan came into the sitting room and made their way around the two of them standing just inside the doorway. Their father had scrubbed his face, but the coal dust that was lodged in the creases around his eyes and mouth was still visible. From his eyebrows up he was dust free because of his cap. Rhodri greeted Orville into their home with a pat on the back.

"Oh, you're in for a real treat, boyo. My Mari's the best cook in town," Rhodri boasted.

He went on to tell Orville that his family name was Welsh too. Orville marveled at Mr. Evans talking to him like he was a regular person. He had no idea that Jenkins was a common Welsh name. Mr. Evans went on to tell him about all of the Jenkinses that he grew up with back in the "old country" as he called it. Mari rolled her eyes and automatically, without thinking, shot a dirty look in Rhodri's direction for talking so familiarly with Orville. Rhodri discreetly raised his eyebrows back at her in rebuke. She understood and tried to be kind to their guest from that moment on. Mr. Evans' kindness had eased some of Orville's apprehensions, but he was still leery of how Mrs. Evans would receive him. Mari had everything ready and on the table. Geraint asked his mother where she wanted Orville to sit. She thought to herself that she would like him to be sitting at his own house and not hers, but she instructed Geraint to seat him in between him and Dai. Everyone sat down. Orville looked around the table at the meal that was before him. The potatoes and the vegetables were in their own bowls. The meat was nicely laid out on a platter. The freshly baked bread sat with a clean tea cloth gently folded around it with the corners overlapping on top to keep it fresh and warm. He had never seen the likes before. He was used to fending for himself. His mother never seemed hungry enough to go through the trouble of preparing a proper meal. On the infrequent occasions when she did cook, whatever was left over remained on the stove for days. No one put anything away. Orville was used to moving the dirty pots and pans around with the rotting food still in them to make something for himself to eat. When he was desperate, he would open a tin and eat out of it rather than trying to hunt up a clean dish or pan to warm up whatever he was lucky enough to find fending for himself.

The kitchen window was open, allowing the lacy

sheers to softly sway with the breeze as the last light for that day was brightly shining in. The room was clean and welcoming. Mr. Evans led the family in prayer. Everyone automatically bowed their heads. Orville followed their lead but kept his eyes open looking around the table as he spoke. As soon as the "amen" sounded, Mr. Evans began doling out the food. He served Orville first, explaining that he was a guest in their home. The aroma was marvelous. He began shoveling down his food as though there were no tomorrow. He did not realize that he was doing it until he reached for his glass of milk to wash it all down and noticed everyone staring at him in amazement. He was so embarrassed that he began to choke on his milk, his face turning redder than the beets that were on his plate. Mari jumped up and lifted Orville's hands above his head until he regained his composure. He couldn't believe he had made such a spectacle of himself within the first few minutes of the best meal he had ever had.

"Ah, don't worry about it, boyo. We just never saw sparks flying off the eating irons like that before. If we were having a contest, I do believe you'd be the winner," Mr. Evans said with a chuckle in his voice.

Mari responded, "You can eat as much as you like; I made plenty. All my boys are big eaters, especially that one. I'm always having to warn him to stop when he gets to the pattern," she said pointing at her husband. They all laughed as they finished their meal at a normal pace. As soon as their meal had ended, Geraint asked if he and his friend could be excused from the table. As soon as permission was gained all the boys got up from the table and gathered in the sitting room anxiously waiting for Mr. Evans to retrieve the beloved scrapbook from the drawer in the sideboard. Geraint was very excited about having his friend over.

"Hey, could yah give us some breathing room?" Geraint snapped, elbowing his brothers in the ribs. Mr. Evans had walked into the room just as the incident occurred.

"Geraint, go see if your mother needs any help in the kitchen."

Orville then jabbed Geraint in the ribs as he was getting up, and whispered, "Ha, woman's work."

"Shut yah gob," he said in retort as he left to see if there was anything he needed to do. There wasn't, and he was back in a flash.

"Ma said she didn't need me."

Actually the gist of what she had said was that she thought that he had already done enough for one day. He was not sure to what she was referring, so he took it for what he wanted to hear, and rejoined his friend in the sitting room. Mr. Evans had the boys gather around the ottoman in the center of the room. He then set the book down with reverence. They gazed upon it as though it was a holy relic that would shoot out beams of glorious light as it was opened, illuminating the room. Mr. Evans gave Orville the honor of opening it to the first page. There was a thick postcard-looking photograph of some young men wearing long sleeved striped shirts with shorts and high socks. The back row was standing while the front row was crouched down on one knee. There were two older men wearing suits standing on either side of the team. A large oval ball lay on the ground, front center of the photograph. As Orville studied the photo, Mr. Evans pointed to the young man that was kneeling on the ground just behind the game ball.

"That's me," he bragged.

"Oh yeah, I see yah now. Where was this?" Orville inquired.

"That's back in Wales when I played rugby, and that's the first team I played for."

"Oh, rugby." Orville never heard of the game before.

Dafydd asked his father to tell Orville the story about the first game that he had played in. Geraint and Morgan urged him on even though they knew the story verbatim.

"Yeah, Dad, tell 'im the story," they pleaded.

Orville did not know much about Wales, and even less about rugby, but he thoroughly enjoyed all the attention he was getting from Mr. Evans, although he struggled to understand his

Welsh accent. It was especially difficult when he got excited and spoke quickly. The Evans boys had lost their accents, but Mr. and Mrs. Evans spoke as though they had just arrived in America. Orville asked Mr. Evans what had happened in his first game. His inquiry caused Rhodri's eyes to light up with enthusiasm. He felt as though he were in his twenties again and just stepped onto the pitch for the first time and he wanted you to be able to visualize what had taken place with him. Mr. Evans proceeded to tell all the stories that his boys knew and loved. Even though they had heard them hundreds of times, they never grew old to them. With every page, there was another photo and another amazing story. Orville hung on his every word. Mrs. Evans did her best to keep Catherine in the room with her while her husband entertained the boys in the other room. She did not see the point of Catherine getting too close to someone who would never be allowed over again.

She could hear her husband still talking as she went up to put Catherine to bed for the night. She decided to do some ironing before she went to bed, anything to stay out of the sitting room. In a way, she was glad that Rhodri liked to talk because he had kept Orville quietly amused. It was dark now and she was hoping that no one would see him leaving their home. She had no idea if anyone had seen him while he was standing out front.

As she was ironing, she could overhear her husband's conversation in the other room. He was just starting a story about when he worked in the coal mines back in Wales, and from what she was overhearing, she knew exactly where he was at in the scrapbook. He had not even gotten to the baseball section yet. She shook her head knowing this would take a while. She had plenty of time to finish any chores needing to be done, and then some.

"That's right, I worked the mines. Once a year they would hold an all-day sporting event. Companies from all over the valleys would send their athletic teams to compete for prizes. Well anyway, I won a ton of prizes; fortunately, one of the prizes was a sort of duffle bag. I stuck everything I won that day into it. I had a china set for four. I was going to give that to my mother. I also won a silver cup for a relay race, and a silver plate for the hundred yards. There were a few other odds and ends shoved in the carryall; I can't remember everything I won that day now. Anyhow, I was on my way home when a policeman grabbed me and started to rough me up. He wanted to know where I stole the stuff. I tried to explain that I didn't steal anything and that I won it all. "Likely story,' he said as he grabbed me by the collar and dragged me through the streets, thumping me on my head all the way to the station. I told him where I worked. So he locked me up and sent another cop over to check out my story. When he got back he told him that Mr. Girling was mad as hell for being awakened and that it had better never happen again. And yes, I won all of it. He had to let me go, but he warned me that if he ever saw me running around in the middle of the night on his beat, he'd give me a proper thumping. He tossed my bag at me and told me to get my arse the hell home. As I left, I overheard them saying, 'He must be fast as shite.' And let me tell yah, boyo, I was." Mr. Evans boasted.

They turned the page, and there it was, baseball. Just like the boys had said. Orville's eyes opened wide as he looked over each card and article. Finally, a sport he knew something about. Mr. Evans had collected the cards from the packages of Old Judge Cigarettes. One of the cards was of Roger Connor. He was the first baseman for the New York Giants. He scored 136 home runs in his career and broke the record. Orville couldn't believe the cards that Mr. Evans had collected. There was a Pete Browning card. He was the Gladiator of the Louisville Eclipse and was best known for breaking his favorite bat. It happened that a man named Bud Hillerich made a bat exclusively for Pete. He used it during his next game and went three for three, and from then on, refused to use anything else. Bud had made a name for himself with that endorsement, and agreed to make all his bats. He also began mass-producing them. He named the bats after Pete. He called them Louisville Sluggers.

The next card was that of Charles Comiskey. He played for the St. Louis Browns. There was a Billy Sunday card. He played center field for the Chicago White Stockings when he left baseball to become an evangelist. Next was Amos Rusie, pitcher for the New York Giants whose fastball was so powerful the catcher used to line his glove with a piece of lead to protect his hand from the impact. Orville turned the page and there it was, a genuine Rube Waddell, his hero. On the next page was a clipping about the 1909 World Series, which was a face-off between two of the greatest baseball players in history. It was billed Honus vs. Cobb. Honus was Geraint's hero. His name was John Peter Honus Wagner, better known as the Flying Dutchman. He played for the Pittsburgh Pirates. Ty Cobb played for the Detroit Tigers. It was the first time in history that a World Series was not decided until the seventh game. Honus stole six bases including home, and batted a whopping 333, while Cobb batted 231, and only stole two bases.

Pittsburgh beat Detroit that year and all of Pennsylvania rejoiced over the win, especially the coal miners. Before Honus played for the Pirates, he, too, was a coal miner.

They went through the entire book, laughing, joking, and swapping stories. Orville had a wonderful time and wished that the night would last forever; unfortunately it was late, and he knew it was time to say "goodnight." He thanked Mr. Evans for allowing him over and asked him to thank his wife for him too. He hadn't seen hide nor hair of her since they ate dinner. After saying his goodbyes he walked out into the night. The warm and welcoming feeling that was kindled inside of him at the Evans home was quickly fading with each and every step. The closer he came to his own house, the more distant it all seemed, until alas, it was like a dream that he was fond of, and if he allowed himself, could think of and smile about from time to time.

By the time he walked through the small broken gate leading into his yard and approached his own front door, that nice feeling was completely extinguished. It was replaced by anger and uncertainty. The reality of his existence came crashing down upon him as he looked into the kitchen and saw his father slumped over in his chair with his head resting on the table, fast asleep. Apparently, the bottle of gin he was nursing had gotten the better of him again. His bottle of booze was gently nestled in the palm of his hand, as though it were the love of his life. Orville had no idea where his mother was.

"Geraint was right," he thought to himself, "they didn't even care that I was gone."

He knew there was happiness in the world to be had, but he realized it would always be for other people, not for him. He knew he was not important to them, but he was angry that even Geraint knew his parents didn't give a flying shit about where he was. He went up to his dirty little room and slammed the door shut. He hoped that the noise would disturb his parents, but it didn't. He picked up some empty food tins, books, plates, and anything else that was handy and threw them against the wall. He then punched the wall as hard as he could with his fist, putting yet another hole in it. Still the house was dead calm. A short time after his tantrum, he gave up the fight, lay down on the pile of dirty clothes that was all over his mattress, and went to sleep.

miners oil wick cap lamp and pick axe

five

PRICE OF COAL

The first morning light was just beginning to filter through the house as Mari made her way down the stairs to begin her new day. She lit the stove in the kitchen and pumped some water into the kettle. Rhodri surprised her coming in from the back yard with paper in hand. She was not even aware that he was awake yet. He sat down at the table, and she instinctively set a cup of tea in front of him. Without saying a word, she finished preparing their breakfast. She could hear some movement upstairs in the children's room and knew that within a few minutes everyone would be gathered at the table. Everything was now ready. She set the food on the table and sat down to enjoy her cup of tea. She heard someone coming down the stairs; it was Catherine. She walked straight to her father and nudged her dark curls under his paper and peered at him with her big blue watery eyes.

"Good morning, sunshine," he said putting the paper aside to pick her up. "Are the boyos up yet?" he asked her.

She rubbed her eyes and yawned, but gave no response. She was still half asleep and he knew it usually took her fifteen minutes or so to wake up enough to talk. He kept her in his lap as he went back to the paper. Dafydd and Geraint came running down the stairs through the kitchen and out the back door to the outhouse, grabbing at each other's nightshirts trying to get ahead of the other. When they got to the door they discovered that Mr. Hennessy was already inside, and even though it accommodated two, and they really needed to go, they did not dare disturb him. He had already yelled at them for trying the door with him inside They danced around the yard until he came out.

When Mr. Hennessy saw how badly they wanted inside, he stopped at the door and tried to talk to them about things he couldn't care less about. He just wanted to see them squirm for a while. They danced around him like water in a skillet of hot bacon drippings. He finally moved away from the door and allowed them entrance. They rushed in together. Their pride left them quicker than they could lift their nightshirts to pee. Sean was laughing to himself as he walked up the path to his back door. As soon as the boys finished they came back into the kitchen and sat down to eat. They were just finishing when Mrs. McDonald came to the front door and knocked. She was the local prophetess of doom. She took it upon herself to report to the townies every bit of juicy gossip that happened. The locals would say telegraph, tele McDonald. Even with her bowed back, she was still a gangling woman who always wore a dark-colored frock with a tattered shawl slung over her shoulders, adding to her gaunt appearance. Even the cane that aided her was black, bent, and gnarly.

"My goodness gracious, you're up and about early today," Mari proclaimed walking to the door to invite her in. "Is everything all right?" Mari inquired, knowing that something must have been wrong or else she would not have come over. Usually, the first words out of her mouth were, "Guess who died, Mrs. Evans."

"Oh," she said with a sigh, "I'm feeling peely wally, but I expect I'll live, unlike some other poor unfortunate, God rest her soul." She finished by touching her forehead, chest and shoulders, making the sign of the cross.

"Come sit down." Mari offered Mrs. McDonald a Welsh cake, or a bakestone as she called it, and a cup of tea. A Welsh cake is about the size of a muffin and usually has currants in it. It is cooked on a hot plate or griddle and browned on both sides.

"Thank you, but no. I don't think I could eat a single bite after knowing what happened at the old Jenkins place last night. I will have some tea though. It might settle my stomach."

Mari had an overwhelming impulse to bombard her

with questions but she stopped herself. Rhodri stood up apologetically and offered his chair.

"Come on, boyos, let the ladies enjoy their tea in peace," he said to the boys as he walked out of the kitchen.

Mari thanked him for his consideration. He was only too happy to oblige. He detested gossip, as did Mari, usually, but not this time, this time she was intrigued. She knew Orville was a bad lot, and whatever Mrs. McDonald knew might vindicate her harsh feelings toward him. Rhodri refused to judge him on what his family had done in the past. He felt everyone had to make his own way in life no matter what the circumstances were. He confided in her that he felt sorry for the boy, and in his own words, "That boy's got an outhouse of a life, and God handed him a corncob."

She knew what he meant by the inference, but she did not agree with it. In her opinion, without exception, trash breeds trash.

As soon as they were alone, Mari leant forward in anticipation. Her eyes opened wildly and even her breathing deepened. Mrs. McDonald was savoring every moment, as Mari was chomping at the bit.

"Oh, I'm glad he took the wee ones with him. They don't need to hear about such goings-on. Little pitchers have big ears, yah know," Mrs. McDonald whispered with one hand cupped around her mouth. "You've got a good man, not like that Frank Jenkins. He's just plain evil. I swear the devil himself won't know what to do with the likes of him," she said taking a sip of her tea. "Lovely, lovely. It's just what I need to calm my nerves."

Mari was not interested in how lovely she thought the cup of tea was or that she was feeling peely wally. She just wanted her to get down to the nitty gritty of the story.

"You said God rest her soul. Did somebody die?" Mari asked wanting her to get to the point.

"Oh my yes, and from the tale told, I wouldn't wish what happened to her on a dog," Mrs. McDonald confessed.

"It was Ethel, wasn't it," Mari concluded.

Mrs. McDonald nodded her head, acknowledging that she had guessed correctly as she lifted her cup for another sip.

"You know how they carry on over there. I guess something like this was bound to happen eventually," stated Mrs. McDonald.

"Something like what?" Mari asked, wanting to strangle the story out of her.

Mrs. McDonald could see that Mari was growing impatient. She had her right where she wanted her, and she relished the moment.

"Mrs. Jones told me they had a real donnybrook over there last night, and that Frank Jenkins beat that poor woman from pillar to post, which, from what I've heard, wasn't unusual," she told Mari as if she had never heard the rumors.

"I know, I've heard the same. I don't know why women put up with that kind of nonsense," Mari said, thinking more about Cate and her life with Sean.

"I don't know why either," agreed Mrs. McDonald.

"So what happened? He beat that poor tiny woman to death?" Mari questioned, wanting more details.

"If only that was all there was to it. No, no, no, it was much worse than that. Mrs. Jones said it was the most gruesome thing she ever had the misfortune to witness, and I know I'll have nightmares about it, and I wasn't even there," Mrs. McDonald stated with a shudder.

"What in the world did he do to her?" Mari asked, not being able to imagine what had happened.

Mrs. McDonald told her, "Well, I guess after he beat her he wasn't done. He wanted to humiliate her too, as if she wasn't humiliated enough, the bastard. I guess they had a fire going in the front yard for some reason, who knows, anyhow, he started burning all her clothes."

"Duw, why would he do that?" Mari asked.

"Because the man is insane, especially when he drinks, and he is always drunk. I suppose Ethel was trying to stop him when he began ripping the clothes right off her back and was trying to burn them too. Poor thing was standing outside naked as a jaybird. I guess he was so loud and drunk he woke up the entire neighborhood. Well you can just imagine with that kind of a ruckus going on. Anyway, he started calling everyone over to see his wife the whore," she told her.

Mari was sitting in awe, shaking her head as Mrs. McDonald told her the rest of the sordid details. It was not a surprise that a Jenkins was involved, but it was still a shock to hear the story.

"I can't imagine Ethel standing there taking that. Why didn't she just go inside?" asked Mari.

"Ah, she was probably just as drunk as he was," claimed Mrs. McDonald.

"So for heaven's sakes, how did she die?" Mari asked again.

Mrs. McDonald crossed herself and went on with the story, "Dorothy said that everyone thought the fight was over and started going back inside when, out of the blue, he picked her up and tossed her into the flames, like she was a piece of rubbish. Dorothy said that the image of Ethel trying to get out of the fire will haunt her till the day she dies. Ben Miller and Ezra Johnson ran over to help, but it was too late to save her. They pulled her charred naked body out and placed a blanket over her. By then the police were there, too late, as usual. I guess old Frank was kicking and screaming as they dragged him off to the pokie, saying that she was nothing but a backstabbing wicked woman and that she got just what she deserved."

"Duw, duw, duw, how awful. Where was Orville during all this?" Mari asked.

"God only knows where he was when the fight started, but I guess he did make it home around the time the police was dragging his father off kicking and screaming. You know he probably could have stopped this from happening if he were there, but no, he had to be out running the roads looking for trouble, when trouble was right in his own front yard," she said out of disgust.

"I don't care if he was drunk or not. How could a man

do something so awful to anyone, let alone his own wife!" Mari questioned in unbelief.

"Frank Jenkins is not a man; he is the devil himself. He will be the one in the flames of hell as soon as he is tried and hanged for what he did to his poor wife. Yeah, he will swing for sure, and good riddance to him, too."

Mari knew that there was no way to protect her children from hearing about such a heinous act. It was the first murder that ever took place in New Salem, and she was sure the story would remain in the local papers until after the trial was over. It was the biggest story to hit the small town since that of little Ben Bauer and the local children who abandoned him to die after his accident with a train.

The details of the murder could not be quelled. Everyone heard what had happened at the old Jenkins place and was talking about it. Ethel Jenkins was laid to rest in the local cemetery. Orville stood outside the gates and watched as his mother's coffin was lowered into the ground. He watched as the grave diggers filled the hole. When they finished, they patted the mound of fresh dirt with their shovels a few times and set a block with a number on it, marking the grave site. There would be no headstone with Ethel's name on it, no flowers to show she was loved by anyone, no preacher to say a prayer over her grave. There was just a mound of dirt that, as time went by, would settle back into the earth and become just another grassy knoll that eventually would sink down to the same level as the older graves there.

The day that Ethel was buried, Frank Jenkins hung himself in his cell, saving the town from a costly trial. Orville considered it the most decent thing that his father had ever done. Orville kept to himself after his parents met their untimely deaths. He quietly took a job in the mines and moved from the family home into company housing. It was easy for him to make the transition to working in the mines. They were dark enough that he would not be noticed, and it was loud enough so he could not think about what happened. He felt he had just moved from one dirty pit into another. He was thankful; at least, this pit paid him a wage. One clear, crisp September evening, the night sky turned amber by the flames of the old dilapidated Jenkins home burning to the ground. No one bothered to try and put the fire out. The town suspected Orville was the culprit who started the blaze, but no one questioned him about it. The town was relieved to have the eyesore gone.

Fall turned into winter and winter to spring. Remnants of the dusty gray snow melted with every shower. The women of the town were busy with their spring cleaning, but they still made time to roll their eyes and whisper every time Orville walked by. He did his best to ignore their contempt, but found it difficult to deal with. He did not get to spend time with Geraint anymore, but he often thought back on the time that he was invited to his house and how enjoyable that evening was. He would sometimes walk up to Geraint's house after work, but he did not dare go up to the door. He wanted to, but he knew it would just cause problems for the Evans family, and he never want to do that. They were the only people in town that he truly cared about. One evening after Orville had stopped in front of the Evans home, Kelly Hennessy came out and nearly walked right into him. He watched her as she approached him. He could tell that she had not seen him standing there. It was dark and her head was down. As she neared he could tell that she was crying.

"Are you all right?" Orville asked with genuine concern.

It startled her when he spoke, not knowing anyone was there. She stumbled over what she should say in response, being embarrassed to be caught crying in public when she thought she was alone.

"I'm sorry, it's none of my business," Orville said, sensing she was uncomfortable speaking to the likes of him.

He apologized and turned to walk away.

Kelly stopped him and apologized for being caught in such a state, and wiped her eyes. He repeated his question and asked again if she was all right. She assured him that she was fine, but he knew better. He also knew that it would be best if they were not seen standing in front of her house talking, so to protect her reputation he suggested that they take a walk. To his surprise she accepted and they quietly talked as they walked. They ended up at the baseball diamond and sat in the concession stand, where she opened up to his surprise and began confiding in him stories about her father. She told him things that she had never told a living soul. To her amazement, Orville told her that he had already worked out what kind of man her father was before she had said a thing about him.

"How could you possibly know what he's like?" she questioned in disbelief.

"Ah, you forget, I work with the man," he reminded her.

"Even so, I can't imagine he'd show his wicked side at work," she argued.

"He doesn't really, but I can see it's there. I knew he was like my old man. I can't tell you how I knew, but I knew," he explained.

The feeling of relief flowed over her like a cleansing spring shower. He not only believed her, he understood how she felt. They talked for hours. She was able to unburden herself, for the first time in her life, and it felt wonderful. She told him about the horrible names her father would call her when he was angry and that he was always mad about something. Kelly explained that she felt as though she was suffocating. She told him that she often sneaked out of the house after her parents were asleep. Orville began growing concerned about the time.

"I better get you home. I sure as hell don't want your old man to wake up and wonder where the hell you are," he told her.

Kelly did not want to go, but knew he was right. He only walked her half way home so they would not be seen together. He instructed her that when she got home she should go inside through their back door. That way, he explained, if anyone was awake she could use the excuse that she was coming in from the outhouse. She was embarrassed by his mention of her having to use the outhouse as an excuse. He apologized to her for being so crude.

She had often sneaked out of the house, but she had never stayed out so late before. She was scared that she might get caught, so she followed his instructions and was able to sneak in without incident. Before they parted company, they concocted a signal so they could meet in secret again. Each morning as Orville walked to the mines he passed the lot where his old house once stood. The old broken gate still remained, even after the fire. He told Kelly that if she wanted to talk, all she had to do was tilt the gate open as she walked by. He would then check for her signal on his way home from work. When they had the opportunity, they met at the concession stand. It was their secret place. He would anxiously wait for her to give him the signal. He walked home from work in anticipation of their next rendezvous. They usually met once a week, sometimes twice. Orville sometimes had to wait for an hour or two before she would be able to join him. Their love for one another grew as a tender young plant in need of more sunlight. They would have loved to tell the world about their new found love, but they knew it was best to keep it to themselves. Kelly was fearful of how her parents would take the news, especially her father. Orville had a difficult time listening to her talk about the abuse she had to endure at home. He would have liked to have killed her father for the things he put her through, but he thought that if he allowed himself to do something like that, he would be no better than his father was, and he knew he was better than him. He just wanted to keep her safe and protected. For the time being, they needed to be content with the fleeting amount of time that they were able to spend together until they could leave New Salem for good. That was Orville's plan, but Kelly was not ready to leave her mother, and she was afraid her father would only end up taking all of his frustration out on her mother and Ann if she was not there. She felt completely torn.

News of The Great War was increasingly worrisome. Those that immigrated from the old country knew that their friends and family left behind were already involved in the conflict. America began gearing up for the inevitable. As the war escalated, it was apparent that the German Confederation had a ravenous penchant for power and destruction. When the news concerning the attack on the shipcalled Lusitania made headlines, America was stunned. Looking back on the fortuitous demise of the Titanic some three years earlier was one thing; this heinous act was something entirely different. An intentional act of war against civilians was unforgivable. The Titanic started her voyage from England bound for America, where as the Lusitania started her voyage in America and was bound for England. She carried 1,906 souls including 651 crew members. The date was May 7, 1915. The voyage had gone smoothly until she was spotted in the crosshairs of a German submarine off the coast of Ireland. The U-boat fired two torpedoes into the hull of the British ocean liner. She sank within twenty minutes of their impact. One thousand, one hundred and ninety-eight people lost their lives, including one hundred and twenty-four Americans. After the sinking, Germany had the audacity to strike a commemorative medal depicting the event. This single eventcreated sporadic rioting in areas of London.

In spite of all this, President Woodrow Wilson was still resolved to maintain a position of neutrality. His desire was for America to oversee peace talks. Because of his platform on the war, he regained his re-election to office. Rhodri and Mari were nervous about Geraint. He was nearly seventeen now and, in spite of President Wilson's dogmatism, they were fearful that America would end up joining in the war effort anyhow. If that was the case, it would not be any time before Geraint would be drafted unless he was hired into the colliery. Rhodri and Mari agonized over their decision to tell Geraint they wanted him to work the mines alongside his father. Mari thought about all the times she heard a long whistle blow signaling that there had been an accident at the colliery and remembered how her heart sank every time she heard it. All the women of the town would stand on their porches waiting for the Black Maria to come down the street, hoping against hope it was not their loved ones in the back. If a miner was critically injured, instead of attempting the long trip over bumpy roads to the hospital, which even in the best of circumstances was a difficult trip, which many would not survive, the driver of the Black Maria would simply stop in front of a home, allowing the family and local doctor of the injured man in the back, to make him as comfortable as they could until he died. After death, friends and neighbors would clean and dress the newly deceased in his best suit for his wake. Still, Mari looked at the mines as the lesser of two evils in comparison to the war. Geraint was proud to go to work with his father; he assumed they only wanted the extra income he could earn which he was more than willing to contribute. It never crossed his mind that they were just trying to keep him out of the war in Europe. Coal-mining was classified as essential industry. Steelworkers were given the same classification, both being jobs of necessity and very dangerous.

Geraint was on tenterhooks as he walked into the main office for the first time with his father inquiring about a job. Geraint's father warned him that John Sanders was not a pleasant man to deal with, but he was the man to see about working in the mines. To say that he was a hard man would be putting it mildly. His large rotund face was covered with at least a week's worth of stubble. His skin was so rough and pockmarked that it looked as though he shaved his face with a sharp rock instead of a razor. The deep creases around his mouth and down his cleft chin were stained brown from the spittle of the tobacco he chewed. The sour look on his face gave you the impression that the man had never smiled in his life. He stood over six foot tall, and his hands were so large and leathery-looking that they were like baseball mitts. Geraint looked at his hand when he offered it to him to shake. His first thought was that Mr. John Sanders could snap his head off his shoulders with the flick of his thumb as though his head was a dandelion being removed from the stem. Geraint imagined that Mr. Sanders would rather enjoy doing it too. Rhodri could see the fear in Geraint's eyes, so he interrupted and explained why they had come into his office. As soon as his father began speaking to John, Geraint took off his cap and held it in hands. He dropped his head and stared at his shoes. He thought about the times when Morgan would put his blanket over his head thinking it made him invisible. Geraint wished he had the magic to just disappear.

His father nudged him to look at John instead of the floor. Geraint obeyed, taking a deep swallow as he lifted his head. Geraint faced his fear and looked up straight into Mr. Sanders' steely blue, bulging, bloodshot eyes. John studied Geraint's physique, examining him as though he was a horse that he was considering placing a bet on.

"So ya wanna work in the pits like yer old man," John said, spitting in the tin he held. He went on to say,

"Well if you're only half the man he is," pointing to his father, "you'll work out fine."

John Sanders instructed Rhodri to make sure Geraint came in early to get his supplies and orders from the pit boss. John put his hand out for Geraint to shake again, but this time when Geraint put his hand out in response, John pulled him close to him saying, "Now yer Daddy's gonna really see what yer made of, won't he, boy. Yah think I'm tough; wait till yah get in the pit. You'll see what tough is."

Geraint could not wait to get the hell out of there. The man terrified him. The pride that he had felt about working with his father had melted away and was taken over by dread. The very thought of him being a disappointment to his parents weighed heavily on him. He was aware how dangerous the mines were and remembered the close calls his own father had. His mind was flooding with thoughts when his dad put his hands on his shoulder as they walked out of the office. He told him that he was proud of him and not to worry; he would do fine. It was just what he needed to hear. Mari was sweeping the front porch when she saw them coming up the road. It struck her how grown up Geraint appeared walking side by side with his father. For the first time in her life, she saw him as a man instead of her little boy. Rhodri began to chuckle as they approached the house. Geraint inquired as to what he thought was so funny.

"I'll tell yah what, boyo, I almost shit myself when John said 'if you're only half the man'. Let me tell yah, that is high praise coming from him. I always thought the nicest thing he ever did was fart downwind, and that was by accident. I swear, in all my days, I've never heard that man say a kind word about anything or anybody. He's always pissing and moaning about something. You'll see what I mean come payday," his father explained.

"Payday," Geraint said with a smile, slapping his hat in his hands.

"Oh, don't you worry, boyo, you're gonna earn every cent you make. They ain't gonna give you nothing," his father told him.

Mari put her broom away and gathered the family together. Rhodri and Geraint came in laughing and cutting up.

"Well?" she asked.

Rhodri allowed Geraint to answer for himself saying,

"Go ahead, tell 'em, boyo."

"I start tomorrow," Geraint said with a smile.

"Well done," was Mari's response.

Her feelings were still mixed. Her only consolation was that she was sure that he was now saved from being drafted. Prior to the war, Mari was adamant that none of her boys would have to work the mines. She wanted them to have a proper education and work with their minds and not with their backs. Circumstances, in this instance, altered her convictions. Her father had been a coal miner back in Wales. She remembered what a handsome man he was when he was young, before the mine whittled him down. He ended up nearly blind and hard of hearing. His legs had been severely injured during a cave in and he could barely walk. Mari remembered the day her father came home with the fingers from his left hand in his lunch pail. He lost them when his hand was crushed against the wall by a coal cart. Mari never forgot the look on his face when he came through their cottage door that night. He was a ghostly shade of pale which was apparent even through the coal dust that covered him. He slowly walked into the room and sat next to the fire clutching his lunch pail to his chest. The pit bosses did not deem it a serious enough injury to warrant an escort home. They cauterized his hand and sent him on his way fully expecting him to give them a full day's work on Monday, which he did.

She remembered how her mother yelled at him for putting the finger stubs into his lunch pail and wanted to know why he had not just thrown them away. He told her that he did not have the heart to bury them in the cold ground because his hands were always so cold. To Mari's horror, her mother slung his finger bits out of the pail and into the fire that he was sitting next to and scolded him by saying they would never have to feel the cold again. It was the most unpleasant memory she had growing up. Nevertheless, Mari felt she needed Geraint to do this for his own protection. If he continued his schooling, she feared that her son would be drafted into war for sure. She comforted herself by thinking that as soon as the war was over he could quit the mines and get a safe job somewhere else.

Rhodri and Geraint left early the next morning and arrived before first shift. Geraint received his tally number, equipment, and orders. He and his father lit their Davey's safety lamps and walked over to join the rest of the miners that had arrived at the adit. They got into the cart that transported them down and into the tunnels. Rhodri told Geraint that he would introduce him to Norton Scott, the pit boss.

"OK boyo, you're on your own. Good luck, and I will see you later. Them there coal carts don't fill themselves, yah know," his father said pointing in the direction of an empty coal cart.

Norton asked Geraint for his tally number.

"682, sir."

"Don't have to sir me, boy 'cuz that shit don't mean nuttin' down here. You just keep yer ears open and do yer job. There's yer ride, hop in. You're working in Hades today." Mr. Scott pointed in the direction of one of the mine shafts.

Geraint picked his tools up and got into the cart with ten other miners going to the same vein. They were shuttled down into the pit until they came to the main junction where the individual shafts splintered off in different directions. It was a labyrinth of tunnels. Geraint was not sure whom he should follow when they got out of the cart. He approached a fellow miner. "Excuse me, I'm in Hades," Geraint said, asking for directions as to where he needed to be. "Yeah, ain't we all," the fellow miner said as he pointed in the direction of that particular part of the vein they called Hades. Every area in the pit had a nickname along with a number. Black Heart, number 23; The Cell, number 16; The Devil's Bend, number 46; and so on. He heard a familiar voice calling his name as he made his way towards Hades. He looked around. Geraint did not recognize who it was for a second. Orville's face was so black and Geraint's eyes hadn't adjusted to the darkness yet. As soon as he realized who it was that called him he was thrilled. It had been a long time since he had seen his old friend.

"Orville. Jesus, it's good to see yah. How yah been?" Geraint asked.

"Oh I'd be all right iffin I could get these damn mules to mind. I swear they are the most cantankerous animals yah ever did see. Either they're kicking at me or they're trying to pin me against the wall. Well, maybe I'll see yah later. I gotta keep movin.' Iffin I stop, I can't get these sons a bitches going again," he told Geraint as he walked by.

As soon as Geraint made his way to the area in the vein where he needed to be, he dug in and got busy. It was not complicated, just repetitive and arduous. All he had to do was chip the coal into rocks away from the wall and fill the coal cart. They were paid twenty-five cents a ton. The pit boss came through making sure the miners were not slacking off at their jobs. When the coal cart was full, he had it removed and an empty one was brought in to replace it. Geraint would see Orville coming around with the mules to haul the coal carts in and out of the shaft. Each miner as well as the pit boss kept track of how many carts were filled as well as the weight of the coal in them. Geraint was relieved when it came time to take his lunch break.

Orville came around to eat with him.

Orville commented that he was surprised to see him there. He always figured that he would become a banker or something, anything but a coal miner. Geraint told him that the family needed the extra income. "Well you might not be glad you're here, but I sure as hell am. Cuz of all the shit with my old man, no one talks to me down here, and them damn mules aren't much company either. We'll have to do this again," Orville claimed. "Hey, that'll be great," Geraint told him. Their lunch break was now over and it was time to get back to work. The pit boss came up to Geraint and told him that the crew broke their long weight and told him to go up to the supply shack and get another one. Geraint did as he was told. To his dismay, John Sanders was behind the counter. He glared at Geraint as he walked into the office. "What the hell are you doing up here mid-shift?" he demanded. "Mr. Scott sent me up to get a long weight; ours broke," Geraint explained. "Stand over there," he barked. Geraint stood away from the counter as John Sanders was busily going through the books logging figures. He never left the counter, and he did not move to get the tool he asked for. A couple of other men came in asking for this and that; John immediately got what they needed. As soon as they left he stuck his nose back into his paperwork, not even looking in Geraint's direction. Geraint took a deep breath and walked back to the counter and asked if he had forgotten why he was there. "Well, you came in for a long wait, right; well now you've had one. Get back to work," Mr. Sanders told him.

Geraint was fuming about the time he wasted in the office. He couldn't believe they pulled a stupid prank on him like that. He did not say a word to anyone as he went back to Hades to finish up his work for the day. He was still aggravated and somewhat disappointed at shift's end. No one had warned him about such antics. When the whistle blew he secured his tools in his locker, picked up his canteen and lunch pail and left. He met his father as he walked home.

"Well boyo, how'd yah like yer first day? I heard they

sent you up for some supplies," his father said.

"Did you know they were going to do that to me?" Geraint asked angrily.

His father lifted his hands in defense saying, "Hang on, boyo, I wasn't in on it, but I must admit I had a hunch they might try something like that. Just brush it off. You'll laugh too when it happens to someone else.

Hell, you should be flattered. It's kind of a rite of passage," his father told him.

"Oh, so they did it to you too?" Geraint asked, thinking he had been through it too.

"Hell no, they wouldn't dare try that shit on me," he said with a chuckle.

Geraint rolled his eyes and gave a sarcastic, "Thanks a lot, Dad."

They were nearly home when Sean Hennessy caught up with them.

"Hey, how'd yah like yer long wait? Was it heavy?" he said as he slapped him on the back laughing.

"Ah, he was just humoring them. Leave the boy alone," Rhodri told him, knowing Geraint was in no mood to be teased about what happened earlier that day.

"Wait till I tell the girls. Yah know how they are. Tell a graph, tell a woman. I'd have a wager that by noon tomorrow every man, woman and child will know about this one. Right, Rhodri?" Sean said, egging Geraint on. "Yeah, yeah," was all Rhodri said to Sean. "Shite, when you work as hard as we do, it feels good to have a good laugh now and then, hey," Sean exclaimed elbowing Geraint.

Geraint was finally at his own front door. He could not wait to get inside and away from Mr. Hennessy. As soon as he walked inside the house, the aroma of his favorite meal filled his nostrils, pushing the thought of what had just happened to him out of his mind. His mother had prepared his favorite meal as a compensation of his first day in the mines. Fried chicken, mashed potatoes with gravy and something they never ate back in Wales, corn-on-the-cob. Back in Wales they considered corn chicken food and would not touch the stuff. Geraint had never tried it until they moved to America, even then it took some coaxing. She also made some bread and a fresh apple pie. Geraint was in heaven. For the moment he had forgotten all about the prank and Mr. Hennessy. As soon as she was finished putting every-thing in bowls and putting it on the table she called everyone in for supper. Rhodri sat at the head of the table where he normally sat, but this day she instructed Geraint to sit at the other end of the table in her chair. It was quite an honor. Normally, Rhodri would lead any conversation at the table, but that day his father turned the spotlight over to Geraint. It was his first day in the mines and it was the first time he felt like a man. It was a day that he would never forget. He now understood what his father meant by "a rite of passage."

The next morning was the first time Geraint joined his parents in their discussion of the daily news. Rhodri read aloud as Geraint enjoyed his tea . Mari was busy putting the finishing touches on breakfast. She carefully set everything on the table be-fore them and then turned her attention to packing their lunches and filling their canteens.

"What would you like to hear about now? The western front, the eastern front, the Italian front, Palestine, Mesopotamia, the list goes on and on," Rhodri questioned. "I don't know about you, but I would love to hear some good news for a change," Mari stated. He began searching. "Here we go, Luv; it says here that the British along with the Russians are now occupying Per-sia. They wanted to stay neutral, but the Brits were too strong for 'em," he commented. "Well that is good news. I'm glad the Brits got a stronghold somewhere. What a bloody mess," Mari said as she sat down to join them at the table.

Mari stopped talking as she heard Catherine coming down the stairs. "Ah, come here, sweetie, tell your daddy and Geraint goodbye. They have to go to work now."

Catherine rubbed her eyes as she walked over to her father to give him a hug and a kiss.

"Look at that face," he said as he bent down to kiss her. "It could melt snow."

With that, Geraint and his father picked up their canteens and lunch pails and left for work. It was all new to Geraint and yet it already seemed like a familiar routine. He was no longer a boy. It seemed like overnight Geraint Evans walked through the door and into manhood. The world somehow did not seem quite as large as it used to.

six

MISGIVINGS

On a winter's day, in late December, Geraint decided to leave New Salem to do some shopping. The air was crisp and cold, but the sun was brightly shining on his back as he walked to the depot. His errand took him into Uniontown, which was only an half-hour ride by bus. He knew all the local shops and was familiar with the merchandise that was available. He had an idea for some gifts he intended on buying for his family. It was a pleasant trip down the winding roads of Pennsylvania. Geraint looked out of the window of the bus and imagined the excitement on everyone's face as they opened the wonderful gifts he would buy them for Christmas. It was the first time he had earned enough money to do something really extravagant and it felt good. He took his time walking through every shop until he found just the right gift for each person on his list. He bought his mother a beautiful silk, beaded handbag with a tassel which was imported from Paris, France. Geraint bought his father a new shaving kit, also imported, but from Persia. For his brother, Dafydd, he purchased a pocket knife which sported a genuine ivory handle that had an oval, silver plate in the center for engraving a name. Geraint decided on a new baseball mitt and ball for Morgan. For his sister, Catherine, he found a lovely doll that was adorned in a pretty white dress with small blue flowers and a lacy pinafore which was sheer enough to allow the delicate pattern to show through. As Geraint gently picked the doll up to examine it closer, he noticed the petticoat under the dress as well as the frilly socks and buttoned shoes. The store clerk pointed out yet another feature concerning the doll that he hadn't noticed. As she laid the doll backward, its eyes closed as if she was going to sleep and opened again as she brought it back into an upright position. Geraint was sold, he knew that Catherinen would be absolutely thrilled with it. She never had a proper doll before. The shopkeeper wrapped all of his purchases for him.

He was over the moon with joy as he made his way home with his bundles. He had everything ready, but there were still a few days till Christmas. Geraint hid everything he purchased that day under the stairs in the cellar and carefully laid a blanket over the gifts so no one would see the treasures he had found. He could not wait to see their faces as they opened their respective gifts. They set the tree up on Christmas Eve. The candles were carefully placed around the branches. They would light them on Christmas Day. Geraint got up before anyone else and retrieved the gifts from the cellar and slipped them under the tree. He put them way in the back just out of sight. Everyone else in the house was still fast asleep when he had finished. He noticed that his parents had already placed the children's gifts under the tree. Geraint had a pretty good idea what they were, a knitted scarf and probably an orange for everyone. The only gifts that he saw under the tree that he was not sure of were the ones his father and mother would give to each other. He lay down on the sofa waiting for Christmas to begin. He had just fallen asleep when he was awakened by the sound of his mother rattling around in the kitchen.

"Is everyone up?" Geraint asked with anticipation.

"Your father's coming down now. I'm going to make some tea. Would you like some?" she asked him. "I guess so. Are we going to wake everyone up?" Geraint asked his mother excitedly.

"I don't think we'll have to, Luv. As soon as they hear us stirring down here they'll be down; don't you worry. They know it's Christmas," she said, knowing he was excited.

Her suspicion was right. Before she poured the tea into their cups, Catherine, Dafydd, and Morgan were awake and down the stairs too. They gave a "Merry Christmas" to all and went straight into the sitting room where they gathered near the Christmas tree. Their father came in and lit the candles, illuminating the room with a dancing golden glow. After the tree was lit he led the family in prayer and they proceeded to sing a Christmas song. When the singing was over, Rhodri asked Geraint if he would like to do the honors and pass the gifts out one by one. He started with the gifts that his parents were giving to all of their children. Catherine, Dafydd, Morgan, and Geraint opened them. Their mother had, in fact, knitted each of them a scarf and accompanied it with an orange. They thanked their parents for the gifts. Rhodri asked Geraint to give his mother the gift he had bought for her. It was an ornamental hair comb. Geraint thought that it was pretty, but he still thought his was the better gift. His mother said that she intended on wearing it in her hair when they went to church for the Christmas service later that morning.

Mari then gave Rhodri his gift from her. It was a watch fob along with his knitted scarf. The Evans family thought that the gift-giving had ended for the day when Geraint pulled his surprises out from behind the tree. To everyone's delight, he began passing them out one by one, starting with his father's gift. Everyone held their breaths as Rhodri opened the present that was professionally gift-wrapped. What lay beneath the pretty paper was a wooden box. There was a crest burned and stamped into the lid, bearing two arched Saracen swords crossed with a crescent moon and star above them. Underneath the crest were the words: made in Persia. Rhodri opened the lid, revealing a beautifully packed shaving kit neatly tucked inside. Each piece was nestled by navy blue silk that was indented by its shape. The boys gasped as their father showed everyone what Geraint had given him for Christmas. Catherine was thrilled by everyone else's excitement, even though she had no idea what the shaving kit would be used for. There was a ceramic mug accompanied by a round bar of shaving soap, a camel hair brush for the application, along with a new folding straight razor. The kit was stunning. Geraint's siblings' anticipation soared to new heights, wondering what they were going to receive from their older brother. Geraint then presented his mother with her present. As she opened it, she expressed to him that he really should not have spent so much money on extravagant gifts. Her heart sank as she admired the beautiful silk bag with the pretty beads and tassel. She was trying to guess, without saying anything, as to how much everything must have cost him. Catherine was admiring her mother's purse when Geraint handed her a gift with her name on it. As young as Catherine was, she still unwrapped her gift carefully and methodically desperately trying not to tear the pretty paper. She carried on until she could see the doll's face. After that, she recklessly ripped through the paper allowing the pieces to fall onto the floor where she was sitting. She was anxious to see what her new dolly was wearing. Little Catherine was fascinated by the eyes opening and closing as she tilted her back and forth. From the moment she had the doll in her arms, her interest in what anyone else would receive diminished dramatically. She was busy playing with her new gift. Morgan was the next one to be handed a present, courtesy of his older brother. He, too, was excited with his new mitt and ball. Geraint gave Dafydd his gift last. It was the smallest of all the presents. He unwrapped the narrow rectangular box. Inside was the ivory-handled pocket knife. There was an oval plate inlayed in the center with Dafydd's name inscribed on it. His jaw dropped when he laid eyes on it. "But I didn't buy you anything," Dafydd said embarrassed.

"I know that; besides, I didn't buy these because I wanted something in return. I bought 'em because I wanted to. It's as simple as that," Geraint explained. Geraint felt as big as a mountain. His family thanked him for all their gifts, which made Geraint feel proud, but in his opinion, no thanks was necessary. Seeing the enjoyment on everyone's face was the best thanks that he could hope for. Catherine asked her mother if she could take her new dolly to church. Mari informed her that church was not the place for toys and told her that it would be waiting for her when they returned home after the family had properly given thanks to the Lord for the wonderful Christmas that they were enjoying. They ate some breakfast and prepared to leave for Church. Mari suggested to Catherine, just before they left for church, that she lay her new dolly down in the cradle so she could close her eyes and take a nap while they were gone. Catherine thought it was a grand idea and willingly relinquished the doll. Dafydd was the only one that was able to carry his gift with him to the Christmas service. He sat in the pew smiling because he could feel the bulge from the knife against his thigh. The pastor of the church thought Dafydd was smiling because he had the joy of the Lord in his heart. Dafydd thought it was such a grownup gift and could not wait for the opportunity to use it on something. Mari and Rhodri were the only members of the Evans household that actually paid attention to their pastor's sermon; the children were busy thinking about their Christmas presents. They couldn't wait to get back home and paw over them. It was the best Christmas they had ever had, and it was all because of Geraint's generosity.

Within fifteen minutes of the Evans family coming home from church, Morgan asked if he could go outside and play catch with his new mitt and ball. His mother had already yelled at him once for tossing the ball around in the house; nobody wanted to go with him. It was too cold and they had just walked all the way home from church. Rhodri, Mari and Geraint sat in the kitchen talking, while Dafydd, who had found something he could whittle on his way home, sat on the steps that led down to the cellar. Catherine was off busily playing with her new dolly. She thought of a name for her while she was at church; she called her Elizabeth. Morgan went into the sitting room by himself and sat near the Christmas tree. His father's gift was sitting on the floor next to the settee. Morgan decided to examine the shaving kit a little closer. He did not dare touch the mug, soap, or razor; he knew he would catch it for that. He carefully took the brush out of its place and stroked it onto his face, pretending he was going to shave. He heard someone coming and quickly placed the brush back in the spot it originally came from. He then decided to ask his mother if he could go into the cellar and bounce the ball off of the wall for a while. She told him that she would not mind him doing that as long as he was careful and it did not make too much noise. Dafydd went down with him to keep him company. He remembered that Morgan used to be afraid to go into the cellar by himself. Dafydd figured he must have really wanted to play catch so Dafydd got his old mitt and joined Morgan for a while in the cellar. They played until their mother called them up for dinner. It was a wonderful feast and the perfect end to a perfect day. The entire family was worn out by all of the holiday excitement. It had been a long day so they retired early that evening.

Catherine came into her parents' room about three in the morning complaining that Morgan was making her hot. Mari wasn't sure what she meant by that and decided she should go and investigate. Mari was still drowsy when she put Catherine in bed with Rhodri and went into the children's room to check on Morgan. He was burning up with fever. She went back to her room and woke up her husband. She asked Rhodri if he could carry Morgan downstairs and lay him on the settee. She would be able to tend to his needs easier downstairs, plus she was thinking that it was always a little cooler in the sitting room than it was up in the bedrooms. Mari needed to get his fever down. Morgan woke up as his father started to lift him out of his bed. Morgan complained that his head hurt and his throat was sore. He began shivering as though he was cold as soon his father took the covers off him to carry him down the stairs. Rhodri asked Mari if she wanted him to go and fetch the doctor. Because of the early hour, they were not sure what they should do about calling for the doctor. They decided to wait a few hours to see if she could get the fever down. She told Rhodri to go back to bed and that she would call him if she needed him. She wet a tea cloth and placed it on his forehead. As her eyes adjusted to the light, she could see that his face and neck were beginning to swell. He had some blistering about his cheeks. She wondered if someone could get both mumps and chicken pox at the same time. She had never heard of the likes, but she didn't know what to make of it. Rhodri came down a few hours later and asked if Morgan's fever had lowered.

"No, his fever is still high and I am worried. You better

go fetch the doctor," she said.

"What do you think he has?" he asked as he was getting his coat on.

She shook her head looking confused. "I have no idea, but I don't like it one bit. We probably should have sent for the doctor hours ago," she told him.

He too was concerned for Morgan's well being and rushed to retrieve the doctor. Catherine was still in her parents' bed fast asleep. Before their father came in with Doc Pritchard, Geraint and Dafydd woke up and made their way into the kitchen. They saw the light in the sitting room and peeked in and asked their mother for a cup of tea. She raised her hand and shooed them out. There really was not much else she could do for Morgan right then; he seemed to be sleeping comfortably. She nearly told the boys to get their own tea, but figured they would make a mess of it. She decided that she should probably make some for Rhodri and the doctor anyhow. She told the boys to keep their voices down, explaining that Morgan was not well and needed his rest.

"What's wrong with 'im?" Geraint asked.

"He's got a bad fever. Your father went to fetch the doctor," she told them.

"Is he that bad he needs a doctor?" asked Dafydd.

"Do you think I would have sent your father out in the middle of the night if I did not think it was serious?" she snapped.

"I'm sorry. I was just asking," Dafydd explained apologetically.

"I know, Dai. I'm sorry. I am just so worried about him," she said.

She made a pot of tea and some toast for breakfast while Morgan slept. As soon as she had finished, she went back into the sitting room to check on him. The swelling and blisters seemed to be worsening by the minute. She was anxious for Rhodri to return with the doctor. Dafydd and Geraint took care of Catherine when she woke up. Mari told both of them that she did not want any of them in the sitting room, except for her and the doctor, since she did not know whether it was contagious or not. By the time Rhodri came back with the doctor, Morgan was waking up complaining again of a sore throat. It was not too long after the doctor examined Morgan that he felt he knew what was ailing him, but he still did not know how he could have contracted the disease. He began questioning Mari and Rhodri about Morgan having contact with a sick animal. They were not aware of any such contact and inquired what that had to do with what was wrong with Morgan.

"I am going to start him on a treatment of colloidal silver. If it is what I think it is, it might help, and even if I am wrong, it won't hurt. I have seen a case similar to this one, but only once," the doctor confirmed.

"If I am right, we need to figure out the source of the infection. Whatever infected him could easily infect someone else," the doctor explained.

"A similar case of what?" Mari asked.

"It appears he has somehow contracted anthrax."

"Anthrax! Oh my God," Mari cried. "It can't be." The doctor told them that if it was anthrax it would not take long before the infected area would worsen still. He explained that the blisters would ulcerate and turn into black lesions. They began questioning Morgan while he was awake as to how this could have happened to him? Morgan had no idea what could have made him sick. Morgan claimed that he felt really good all Christmas Day.

The doctor questioned Morgan as to why he thought the swelling was only on his face and nowhere else on his body.

"Look at your arms, and legs; they're fine. It is only covering your cheeks and chin; that is where you are infected. Try to remember, boy. Did you recently hug a stray dog or some other kind of animal?" The doctor questioned Morgan trying further to jar his memory while he was still lucid and had the strength to answer. When Dr. Pritchard mentioned cheeks and chin, Morgan thought he might know what it was, but it was not an animal.

"Could it have been my father's new shaving brush?" he asked the doctor quietly, not wanting to admit out loud that he had gotten into it.

The doctor asked Rhodri where the new shaving brush was and if he or anyone else had used it yet. Rhodri handed the whole kit to the doctor, saying, "I don't think so. I just got the damn thing yesterday. Hell, I didn't even know Morgan touched it."

"Let's have a look at it."

As the doctor examined it without touching it, he said, "Ah, a camel hair brush. Well, it looks like we solved the mystery; the camel used must have had anthrax."

"Morgan, what did you do?" his mother asked crying.

"I only brushed my face with it for a minute. I was pretending to shave. I put it right back," Morgan confessed.

"It will be all right, boyo. The doctor said there is a treatment," Rhodri gently spoke trying to comfort his son.

The doctor met with Mari and Rhodri in the kitchen. They told Morgan to close his eyes and get some rest. His mother promised she would be right back. He was tired.

"I think it would be best if you put him into a sanitarium. They will do everything they can to make him comfortable," the doctor told them.

"I will do no such thing. I will take care of him right here. You show me how to treat him, and I will do it," Mari insisted.

"I know you would like to keep him here, but I must warn you, it will be harder than you think. The fever will probably worsen causing the boy to go into convulsions. And besides that, just watching his appearance change is going to be very hard on you. The blisters will turn into swollen black lesions; it can be a nightmarish disease," the doctor warned.

Rhodri and Mari were in shock listening to the doctor describe what was going to happen to their beautiful boy. Rhodri thought that maybe the sanitarium was the best considering the circumstances, but Mari would not hear of it. She was not about to let her son be carted off and allow a bunch of strangers to care for him when he was so sick. Rhodri was not about to argue with her about it; her mind was made up. Mari asked the doctor to show her what she needed to know to make Morgan as comfortable as she could; reluctantly, he informed her what she should do. He told her that he would come over every day with the colloidal silver for treatment; the remainder of his care would rest upon Mari's shoulders. The doctor took the shaving kit with him to burn the brush to eradicate the anthrax. Before he left he told them that they needed to get a hold of the store where it was purchased to see if they had sold any other shaving kits imported from Persia. Catherine Hennessy saw Dr. Pritchard leaving the Evans's home. She was going over to wish them a merry Christmas on Boxing Day. After seeing the doctor, she wanted to make sure all was well. She approached their door to knock, but there was a sign on the door asking everyone to please use the back door. *That's odd,* she thought to herself.

She obliged and made her way down the steps and around the back. Rhodri answered the door.

"Merry Christmas."

As soon as the words came out of her mouth, she wished she could take them back. She could see by his countenance that there was not anything merry inside their house. She could hear Mari crying just inside the door.

"What's happened?" Cate asked concerned.

"Oh Catherine, please, come in. Go talk to your friend; she'll tell you," Rhodri said opening the door for her.

With that, he put his coat on and walked outside. Catherine rushed over and caressed Mari. She stroked her back and began crying along with her even before she knew what had happened.

Mari sobbed. "It's Morgan," was all she could get out. Catherine's heart was in her mouth. "What's happened to Morgan? I saw him yesterday. He was fine.

Did he have an accident?" she asked horrified.

Mari tried to compose herself to explain what was going on.

"The doctor thinks he has anthrax," she said.

"He thinks? So he's not really sure?" Catherine responded with some hope.

"He said that if he is right, we will know before the day's out. He wanted to stick him in a sanitarium!"

Mari told Catherine, still not believing what was happening.

"Is he contagious?" asked Catherine.

"It doesn't matter; I am not sending him anywhere!" she said adamantly.

"Where is he?"

"He's in the sitting room. I'm keeping him away from the other children just in case, but the doctor did tell me we can't catch it just by being near him. Oh Cate, you should see his sweet little face. God, I can't believe this is happening," Mari cried.

Catherine knew that Mari was anxious to go in and check on Morgan's condition. They talked a bit longer before she excused herself and went back to her house. Before she left, she told Mari to call for her if she needed any help and that Morgan would be in her prayers.

Mari took a deep breath, put on a brave face, and went into the sitting room to be near her son. He looked the same as he had when she left him; she hadn't been gone that long. Still she clung to the hope that the doctor was wrong about his diagnosis. Morgan was still burning up with fever, however. She took a bucket and went outside and gathered some snow. She used some tea cloths and wrapped the snow inside for cold compresses, and placed one under the nape of his neck and the other on his forehead. She sat next to him and stroked his small frame with a cool cloth trying to bring the fever down. His sweet little face looked too tender to touch. He was complaining that he was chilled and kept pulling at the blanket trying to get warm. She stayed by his side until he went back to sleep. Rhodri was in the backyard when Catherine came out. She went up to him and hugged him and expressed to him how sorry she was to hear the news, and that he should not hesitate to call her if they needed anything.

Sean was sitting at the kitchen table watching Catherine consoling Rhodri through the window. He jumped all over her with his venomous tongue as soon as she walked into the kitchen.

"Who the hell do you think you are?" Sean demanded.

"Don't you even start with me, Sean Hennessy. I'm not up for it. You have no idea what they are going through, so put a sock in it," she barked back at him.

"All right, Miss. Perfect. You tell me then, what is going on?" he asked sarcastically.

"Morgan is really sick," she said.

"Ah, is the boy feeling peely wally?" Sean said jokingly.

"It is not funny, Sean. The doctor thinks he has anthrax."

"Anthrax? How the hell did he get anthrax?" Sean said in disbelief.

"It was from a shaving brush Geraint bought Rhodri for a Christmas gift," she told him.

"Does Rhodri have it too?" Sean asked.

"No, he hadn't used it yet. Morgan was playing with it, acting like he was shaving," Cate reported the information that Rhodri had told her while they stood in the backyard.

"Well I guess that'll teach 'im. Never touch what doesn't belong to you," Sean said, justifying Morgan's sickness like he deserved it.

"WHAT! I cannot believe you just said that," Cate argued.

She was furious with his attitude. She told him that she was going to go back over after they finished their supper. She wanted to take something over for them. She knew Mari would not be up to preparing a meal. Sean was mad about the fact that she was going to take food out of their mouths and give it to the neighbors. He left and walked up to the pub for a few hours. Catherine broke the news to the girls after he left. They were visibly shaken. Catherine had their supper ready when Sean came back. She was angry that he stayed so late at the pub. She really wanted to check on how the neighbors were faring, but she was afraid to leave the girls at home in case their father came home looking for a fight. She was afraid to take the girls with her just in case the doctor was wrong about the anthrax and Morgan was contagious. It turned out to be a good thing she waited for Sean. Just as she thought, he came in looking for a fight, and he got one. They had just sat down at the table. They bowed their heads as Sean said grace. He even put Morgan in his prayer. The amen was just out of his mouth when he started in on Kelly.

"Looks like the sad news hasn't affected your appetite," he said, goading Kelly.

"Please do not start," pleaded Catherine.

"Why aren't you eating?" he demanded of Ann.

"I'm not very hungry," she said quietly.

"You had better eat everything that is on that plate. I work too damn hard for the likes of you to let that food go to waste," he yelled.

Ann tried to eat, but all she was doing was pushing her food around the plate fighting back the tears.

He watched her as though he was a hungry snake getting ready to spring on an unsuspecting mouse. He yelled at her a second time about letting her food get cold.

"Look at your sister. Do you think there will be a scrap of food left on her plate? The whole world could crash in on her and she would still eat," Sean told Ann.

Ann stood up in defense of her sister, defying her father. Sean became furious with Ann and grabbed her by the hair and slung her to the floor. He ordered her up to her room. As she ran away crying, he kicked at her.

Kelly stood toe to toe and challenged her father.

He put his fist up as though he would punch her in the face. Catherine jumped between the two of them, yelling at Kelly to go to her room. Sean was egging Kelly on, claiming that he had waited a long time to give her what she needed. Sean resorted to name-calling, as he usually did. "Fat pig" was only one of the choice names he would call Kelly. She ran into the sitting room, grabbed her coat and ran out the front door into the night. She did not care that her mother was calling her. All she could think of was that she wanted to be away from there and with Orville to let him know what was going on. Kelly quietly sneaked around to the back door of Orville's new house.

Orville was shocked when he saw her standing outside. He immediately brought her inside out of the cold. Kelly had never been so brazen as to show up at his door before. Orville never had company, not at his new home or his old family home which he burnt to the ground after his mother's murder. Kelly told him what had happened. Orville wanted to kill her father. Kelly stayed there that night. Orville had to work the mines in the morning, as did her father. Later that morning, Kelly sneaked back into her own home through the back door after she knew her father had left for work. She had become very good about coming into the house quietly. She had done it so many times before. Kelly lied to her mother about where she had been all night. Cate hadn't slept at all that night because of worry. Kelly made up the excuse that she had spent the night at a friend's house.

She explained that her parents were unaware that she was there, so that there was no need to check. Catherine believed the story and was relieved to see her home. She scolded her and told her never to run off like that again.

She complained that she had enough on her mind dealing with what was happening to Morgan. Cate went next door, praying that he had improved in the night. Dafydd was in the kitchen keeping his sister occupied. She asked if their mother was in the sitting room with Morgan. Dafydd nodded.

"She has been in the sitting room all night," he told Mrs. Hennessy.

"How is little Morgan? Has he improved at all?" she asked Dafydd.

"I don't think so. Do you want me to tell my mother that you are here?" he asked.

"Yes, if you could. I would like to see how they are doing," she said.

Dafydd got up and went to the archway leading into

the sitting room. His father had hung a blanket for a door. He peeked in and told his mother that Mrs. Hennessy had come over.

"All right, tell her I will be right there," she said needing a break.

When Mari came into the room, she looked completely frazzled. Catherine put the kettle on for some tea.

"How is he?" Cate asked, afraid that she already knew the answer to her question.

Mari shook her head. "He's worse. I'm afraid the doctor was right. It is anthrax for sure. Everything he said would happen is happening. Oh Catherine, what am I going to do?" Mari said as she started to cry again. Mari asked Dafydd to take little Catherine upstairs so she and Mrs. Hennessy could talk. Mari told her that the doctor had already come around to examine Morgan, and there was now no doubt as to what they were dealing with. It was definitely anthrax. Mari told Cate that she would not even recognize him. His face had ulcerated and swollen twice its normal size and was covered with black lesions. She said that, so far, the treatments that Dr. Pritchard was using were not working.

"I wished Geraint never bought that damn gift," Mari cried.

"Now Mari, you can't blame Geraint for what has happened," Cate told her.

"I know, but I keep thinking who did he think he was, Rockefeller, buying all those expensive gifts?" Mari complained.

"I am quite sure that Geraint feels guilty enough about what has happened," Cate said in Geraint's defense.

"I know, I know, I know. Oh, but Catherine, you should see him. It breaks my heart every time I go in there. And, poor Rhodri; he doesn't know what to do. He keeps thinking that it should have been him instead of Morgan," Mari confessed.

"Are you going to put him in a sanitarium now that you know for sure what you're dealing with?" Cate asked.

"Absolutely not! He's better off here with me," she insisted.

"I suppose you're right," Cate said, not really believing that she was right. "Can I see him?" she asked.

"If you really want to. I need to get back in there anyways," Mari told Cate.

Catherine tried not to let the horror show on her face as she approached Morgan. She felt a tightening in her stomach as soon as she saw the condition he was in. His face was so deformed, it broke her heart. He began to convulse as she looked on. Mari held him and cried until he stopped.

"Oh Mari," Cate said, not knowing what to say.

She whispered a prayer for the Evans family. After seeing the shape that Morgan was in, she feared that he would not live till the New Year.

She was nearly right; Morgan Joseph Evans died January 2, 1917; he was only ten years old. Cate helped Mari prepare his body. They washed him and clothed him in his Sunday best. Prior to Morgan's viewing, Mari placed the handkerchief that the boys had wrapped her birthday present in three years earlier over his face. She did not want anyone to remember her sweet baby boy looking like that. Mari wanted everyone to remember Morgan for the lovely child that he was. A small coffin was delivered to the Evans's house. Mr. Evans placed his son's body inside to prepare for his viewing. Mari had to leave the room when it was time to seal the coffin for Morgan's burial. The small box was then carried out by Geraint and his father. Morgan was gently put into the back of the hearse. Rhodri and Mari along with Geraint, Dai, and little Catherine rode along with the coffin in the back of the horse-drawn hearse, or the Black Maria as it was also called. They led the way to the cemetery as the townies lined the street out of respect as they passed by. It was a cold gray January afternoon. It had just begun to snow as they entered the cemetery grounds where Morgan would take his final rest. The Evans family, as well as anyone who knew the family, grieved over their loss.

A few times after the burial, Mari sometimes forgot that her son was gone and would set a place for Morgan, as though he would run down the stairs and sit in his chair at the breakfast table. As soon as she realized what she was doing, she would burst into tears and have to leave the room for a while. She was cleaning out some drawers when she found the wedding ring that her mother gave her for Morgan to use for his wedding day. She was thinking that if only she had remembered the ring was there, she would have buried it with him. Little Catherine would hug her mother and ask her not to be sad. She would try to rebound for her sake, but it was like a canker within her eating away at her heart.

It was at least a month before Mari found herself actually laughing, and it was over something Little Catherine said to her one night. She had asked if she could sleep with them. Mari told her that she could for that particular night only and told her not to get used to it. They went to bed. Catherine wasn't very tired and was in a chit-chatty mood, plus she was having a bit of a problem with being gassy. She would talk some and then fart and went back and forth being extremely gassy.

"Catherine," Mari said, "be quiet and go to sleep."

"That's not me talking; it's my butt," she exclaimed with all sincerity.

Rhodri and Mari both had a chuckle over that. That moment with their daughter was a turning point that helped them over the hurtle of grief. That is when they both understood that there was a reason to go on, in spite of their loss. They needed to move forward, and so they did. Slowly their lives were tenderly and carefully knitted back together. After her mourning, Mari resumed having her afternoon tea with Catherine Hennessy, which was something she had not done since the loss of Morgan.

One morning, a few months after the funeral, Dafydd came into the kitchen and informed his mother that Kelly Hennessy was ill. He told her that she was out back. Mari went out to check on her. She was wiping about her mouth with a handkerchief.

"Kelly, are you all right? Dafydd told me you were ill," Mrs. Evans said concerned.

"I'll be all right now. I've had an upset stomach nearly every day. I get ill and then it goes away," Kelly told her.

"Every day for how long?" Mari inquired.

"A few weeks now," Kelly said.

"Kelly, I hate to ask you this, but when did you last menstruate?" Mari questioned.

Kelly was embarrassed. "Oh, I don't know, I have never kept track really. Why would you ask a question like that?"

"Have you been with a boy?" Mari asked ignoring Kelly's embarrassment.

When Mari asked Kelly that question, the penny dropped; her face became redder with embarrassment.

She then tried to remember when exactly her last menstrual cycle was. She began feeling ill again. Her eyes welted up with tears. Mari gave her a hug.

"Duw, Kelly. Do you want me there when you tell your parents?"

"I can't tell them. My father will kill me," Kelly cried.

"They will be very hurt and disappointed, but he will not kill you, I promise," Mrs. Evans assured her.

"You do not know my dad. He will kill me!" Kelly was truly afraid of what might happen.

"Well, maybe you should only tell your mother for starters and let her help you decide what to do about telling your father, but you have to tell them. This kind of thing just can't be hid for long, you know. Who is the father of the baby?" Mari asked out of curiosity.

"I would rather not say," Kelly said, hanging her head in shame.

"I'll tell you what will probably happen," Mari continued.

"What's that?" Kelly asked.

"Don't you have an aunt or cousin up in Detroit?" Mari asked trying to remember a conversation she and Cate had some time ago.

"Aunt Ruby," Kelly confirmed.

"They will probably send you there to have the baby. Do you remember Beverly Ryan? That's what happened to her," Mari told her.

"I thought she went to a boarding school up north?" Kelly questioned.

"That was the story her family told, but that is not why she left. Unfortunately, Kelly, this kind of thing happens all too often. Go on inside. I think it would be best if you tell your mother now, and you don't have to tell her that I know anything. If you can't bring yourself to do it, I will help you later. Just let me know. If I were in your situation, I would not tell anyone, except my parents, of course, including the baby's father. He has done enough damage, don't you think? The least amount of people who know about this, the better off you will be," Mari advised.

She gave her a final hug and kiss and assured her that she would support her no matter what happened. Kelly was terrified of what her parents' response would be. She just did not have the heart to tell them. She began hoping that something would happen to her so she did not have to face what she had gotten herself into. She wished the ground would just open up and swallow her whole. She thought about if she should tell Orville or not tell him; she wasn't sure what to do. The only one she felt comfortable confiding in for the time being was Ann. Kelly wanted to warn her sister not to do what she had done.

Later that day, Catherine and Mari met for their afternoon cup of tea and chat. Catherine was not upset in the least with her daughter, only with her husband, as usual. Mari could tell that Kelly had not told her about the condition she had gotten herself into, and she was not about to be the one to bring it up. She was afraid that Catherine would be upset that she knew about her daughter before she did. They spoke about their usual topics: the war, their husbands, the work that they needed to do. Mari left Kelly's situation out of their conversation. She decided she would give her a couple of days to think about how she would tell her parents. Mari wondered who the father could have been. The thought of Orville Jenkins possibly being the father never even crossed her mind.

Two weeks had passed and Kelly still had not revealed her secret to her mother. Mari was getting worried. Ever since she knew about the baby she studied Kelly's waistline carefully. She swore that she could see a little pooch. She finally asked Kelly when she planned on telling them what was going on. She warned her again that it was not the kind of thing that you could hide for long. Mari gave her an ultimatum; either she told her mother by the end of the week or Mari would. Kelly agreed that she needed to tell them and soon. She wanted to tell Orville first, even though Mari had advised her not to tell the father anything about the baby. She left the signal at the gate in front of the old Jenkins house. She hoped that she and Orville could run off together and live happily ever after without having to face her parents with the news until she wanted to tell them about it. When Kelly came home after signaling Orville, her mother was waiting for her.

"Do you have something to tell me?" she demanded. Kelly fought off the tears. "What do you mean?" she asked sheepishly.

"Don't you play dumb with me, young lady. I know exactly what's been going on. How could you do this? What is your father going to say?" Cate railed on her. Kelly burst into tears. "I am so sorry."

"Saying you're sorry does not help in the least. As soon as your father gets home and you tell him about this, then you will be sorry. Who's the father?" her mother demanded.

She could not bring herself to tell her. Her mother slapped her in the face and ordered her to her room until she was called. Ann was upstairs as Kelly came into the bedroom.

"I'm sorry, Kelly," Ann said apologetically.

"Sorry for what?" Kelly said crying.

"For telling Mom about the baby," Ann confessed.

"You told her?" Kelly said shocked.

"Well you wasn't going to!" Ann defended.

"I thought it would be Mrs. Evans that spilled the beans, not you. I wish I had never told you," Kelly yelled.

"I wish you never told me too, and I wish I never told Mom. I have never seen her so mad in all my life. If she is that mad, what is Father going to do?" Ann began crying out of fear. Kelly walked over and sat on the bed next to her sister.

"Ah, Ann, don't cry. It's all right. You were probably right. I didn't have the guts to do it, and who knows, maybe she will calm down before Father gets home and she can break the news to him instead of me. Perhaps I'll even live through the night," Kelly consoled her sister.

"Oh don't say that," Ann pleaded.

They comforted one another until they heard the front door slam. They knew their father had come in. Kelly waited with a knot in her stomach for the call.

"SHE'S WHAT!" he screamed as he stomped up the stairs to their bedroom.

Their mother was right behind him.

"You fucking whore! How dare you! Who did this? I'll kill him!" her father demanded.

Again Kelly refused to answer. Fortunately, she had not told a soul; no one knew, not even Orville yet. Her refusal to answer infuriated her father even more. He called her every foul name that he could think of as he slapped her around the room. Her mother stepped in and tried to stop him from hitting her so hard, but because he was so angry, he had the strength of ten men. Finally, Catherine, Ann and Kelly had enough of the beating and, in unison , rushed at him, nearly knocking him backwards down the stairs. They had not planned their attack; it just happened. He caught his balance just before he went arse over tits backwards. Sean was shocked by the action taken against him. He never imagined that they would revolt like that. After he steadied himself, he turned and descended the stairs while screaming out threats against all of them. He promised that Kelly would be, in his words, "out on her ass by morning." He meant what he said and they knew it.

First thing the next morning he escorted his daughter to the bus depot. He bought her a one way ticket to Detroit, and handed her a letter of introduction for her aunt. He told Kelly that if her Aunt Ruby did not want her there, then she had better find somewhere on her own. She was not to come back. He made it perfectly clear that she was no longer wanted in their home or in New Salem. He stayed there until she boarded and told her that he never wanted to see her or the bastard she was having ever again. He told her not to bother writing; as far as he was concerned, she no longer existed as a member of the Hennessy family. Catherine kept to herself for a few weeks. She did not come out for her afternoon tea with Mari. The shame of it all weighed heavily upon her. Mari figured out what had happened. She saw Ann around, but Kelly had disappeared. She did not want to pry, and she knew that when and if Cate wanted to talk, she would tell her all about it. The story the Hennessys told was that Aunt Ruby in Detroit had taken ill and that Kelly volunteered to tend to her needs. After the banishment of Kelly, Ann became increasingly lonely. She often found herself at the cemetery putting wild flowers on Morgan's grave. One dull and rainy afternoon, early that spring, Ann was approaching Morgan's grave when she spotted Dafydd already in the cemetery at the grave site. She was going to leave and let him have his visit in peace when he turned and saw Ann standing there. He quietly invited her to join him. She had some wild flowers in her hand.

"Oh, so you're the one that keeps bringing the pretty flowers," Dafydd figured.

"I hope you don't mind," Ann asked him.

"Mind? Morgan would have loved you bringing him flowers. You know what a crush he had on you," he reminded her.

Ann smiled and said, "He was such a lovely boy; we all loved him. You know, I picture him in heaven with my sisters and brother who died back in Ireland. I'm sure they're great friends by now."

"I'm sure they are," Dafydd agreed.

They talked for a while. Ann rose up as it started to sprinkle with rain once more and told Dafydd that she should probably start heading home. She told him that she had already stayed longer than she had planned and better get home before she was soaking wet. Dafydd stood up and offered to walk with her. She gracefully accepted. Mari saw them walk up the front steps together and part at the porch.

"Well, well. What's all that about?" his mother asked smiling.

"Nothing," Dafydd responded.

"It didn't look like nothing to me," she teased.

"Ah, Ma, I was just walking her home," he explained innocently.

"You know, Dafydd, Ann is a lovely girl. I think you would make a wonderful couple," his mother told him.

"Don't get your hopes up, Mom. When is supper going to be done?" he asked.

"Trying to change the subject, are you?... It will be ready in a little bit," she told him.

Dafydd rolled his eyes, shook his head, and left the room, embarrassed by the whole conversation. Mari chuckled to herself, knowing she embarrassed him. The truth be known, she enjoyed doing it. During his evening meal he started thinking about what his mother had said to him about Ann. She really was a lovely girl; he had just never thought about it before. After dinner he asked his mother if she could teach him to dance. She was thrilled by the request. She asked Geraint if he would like her to teach him too.

"No, thank you; miners don't dance," Geraint scoffed at the thought of being taught anything by his mother.

"Now that is not true. Your father used to dance; in fact, we met at a dance," his mother said, correcting him.

"Hey I still dance, you know," Rhodri said. "Every time a hot ember comes my way, I dance."

"Well, aren't you the funny one," she said looking at her husband. She then turned back to her son. "Dafydd, I would be honored to teach you to dance."

His dance lessons began that evening. Dafydd was a fast learner. The next time he knew there would be a dance, he planned on asking Ann, but first he had to ask her father's permission. Mr. Hennessy had never been anything but kind to Dafydd, so he was not intimidated by the thought of approaching him. When the time came, Mr. Hennessy surprisingly gave his approval. Mari, Catherine and Ann were thrilled. The courtship between Ann and Dafydd began with a dance, just like it had with his parents.

seven

THE BIG SHOW

It had been weeks since Kelly Hennessy mysteriously disappeared from New Salem. Orville was desperate to find out what had happened to her. He had not seen hide nor hair of her since the day she signaled him to meet her. He waited for her all that night and nearly froze to death. He heard Dafydd was courting Ann Hennessy, and figured he could ask Geraint about her disappearance, seeing they were neighbors and Dafydd was dating her sister. Geraint told him that, as far as he knew, she had moved to Detroit to care for a sick aunt. Orville could not believe that she had taken off without so much as a goodbye. He would not allow his emotions to show, especially since Geraint knew nothing about their relationship. He could not ask him for her address; that would only cause suspicion. He hoped he would be the recipient of a letter from her even though his reading and writing skills left something to be desired. She did know his address after all, and if she really cared the way he thought that she did, surely she would write to him. He waited a few months for a letter and decided that he was not going to wait any longer. It was too hard on him every time he saw Dafydd and Ann together as a couple. It only reminded him of how happy they could have been if they were given half a chance. That same week, America declared war on Germany. Orville decided that he would leave the mines and join the Army. He did not care that he was already exempt from the draft. He planned on throwing that status away and enlisting. Geraint was surprised by Orville's plan. He, too, had romanticized about going to war and whipping the Germans. Geraint went home that evening and told his parents about Orville's intention. His mother thought he must have been joking. She said that a Jenkins would not have the guts to go to war. His mother then made the comment, "If he knew what was good for him, then he would stay put and forget about such fool-hearted thoughts!"

The way she lit into Orville, Geraint didn't have the nerve to admit he was considering going with him. He was tired of working in the mines. It was a thankless job. He would much rather go overseas and defend both the United States's interest as well as Britain's. He decided that he should keep his thoughts to himself rather than stirring up a war in his own house.

The following day, Mari and Cate's peaceful afternoon tea was shattered by the sound of a long whistle being blown down at the colliery, signaling that there had been an accident. All of the women in and around town came outside and stood on their porches waiting to see if the Black Maria would bring their loved one to their front door. Mari hoped against hope that everyone had gotten out all right. Cate hoped for everyone, save one. She would not have been heartbroken if Sean did not make it out alive, but she feared that he was too ornery to die and let her live the rest of her life in peace.

Mari told Dafydd to run down to the collier and see what had happened. When he returned about a half an hour later, he reported that there had been an explosion below ground, but he saw that his father and Geraint were safe and sound. Dafydd told her that they would be late because they needed to stay and help until all of the miners were accounted for. Cate asked Dafydd if he had seen her husband while he was there. He told her that he had and he was fine.

"Ah, that's good," she said, but she thought, "Yeah, I knew it; he's too damn ornery to die; oh well, maybe next time," she hoped within herself.

Two and a half hours after the explosion at the collier, the Black Maria was spotted coming up the road and into the company housing district of New Salem. Its first stop was in front of Mrs. Kanfer's house. Dr. Pritchard, with the help of Sam Rivers, the driver, carried her son Peter and her husband Michael inside. Two roads down from there and around the corner, the Black Maria stopped in front of Mrs. McConnell's place. Again Doc Pritchard, along with Sam's help, carried the injured inside. Mari and Cate looked on as they helped John McConnell into his house. The McConnells lived directly across the street from the Evanses and Hennessys. All three were seriously injured, but the doctor was certain they would recover and could more than likely go back to work within a few months. The trip to the hospital was such an arduous trek over bumpy roads that it might have killed one or all three of the men before they arrived. It was the doctor's decision if the injured miners could stand the trip or not. The doctor decided they could not. It would now be up to their families, with help from the doctor, to tend to their needs until they were on their feet again.

Rhodri and Geraint were greatly shaken by the experience. Rhodri had been through a number of accidents in the mines, but he told Geraint that close encounters with death was not something a man would ever get used to. It was Geraint's first explosion since he began working there. He had witnessed a few minor accidents. A broken bone here and there, the loss of a finger, but never anything like what had happened that day. It was the first time he looked death in the face. Geraint was terrified as he witnessed the shaft cave in on top of fellow miners. He considered himself lucky to have survived. The fear on the miners' faces was something Geraint would never forget. That evening there wasn't the usual chatter at the Evans's dinner table. Both Geraint and his father remained quiet, not wanting to talk about what had happened that day at work. Mari and the children respected that and were exhausted from being worn out by worry. Everyone went to bed shortly after they had finished their meal that night. They had eaten later than usual because of the explosion at the colliery.

The next morning it was back to work for the two of them as usual. Geraint could not sleep thinking about what had happened and what could have happened. He considered working in the mines to be far more dangerous than going to war.

Geraint figured that at least in a war you were fully armed to protect yourself against an enemy you could see. In the mines most of the things that could kill you were unseen: poisonous gas, a fault in the shaft, or an explosion that could happen without warning. He felt that you could not fight against such things. Geraint spoke to Orville the next day to see if he was serious about enlisting. He told him that if they enlisted together they could serve together in a pal's battalion. Orville was all for it and asked Geraint if he had talked it over with his parents yet. He said that he would that night, and after they received the wages due them, they could go and enlist together. Geraint's parents were taken completely by surprise when he announced that he was going to enlist in the Army along with Orville Jenkins. Geraint had never seen his mother so adamantly against something he really wanted to do before. His father was not happy about his decision either, but at least he held his tongue. His mother went into a rage.

She told him that she was not about to lose another son and forbade him from joining. He tried to reason with her and explained the way he felt about working in the mines, especially after the explosion that took place just a day earlier. He told her that it was the right thing for him to do, and that as an American, she should be proud of him, instead of being angry. She lashed out saying things that she would later regret, things so awful that she would never admit that she had ever said them in the first place. She turned the fight into accusations about him being impetuous and never thinking things through, and that if it were not for his extravagance Morgan would still be alive. Rhodri tried to stop his wife, knowing ahead of time where she was going, but she was on a tirade and could not be stopped.

The accusations stopped Geraint in his tracks. He was gobsmacked, even though he had always bore his own guilt about the whole episode with the camel hair brush. What had happened to Morgan weighed heavily on him, but he had never even considered that anyone else blamed him too, let alone his own mother. This awakening devastated him. By this point it did not matter what she had forbade him to do; he would enlist just as he had planned, and the sooner, the better. For the first time in his life, he felt awkward and out of place in his own home.

That Friday after he got his pay, he packed some belongings and left without saying goodbye. He met up with Orville and they went by bus into Uniontown to enlist. America had only declared war on Germany less than a week earlier, April 6, 1917. Geraint enlisted just before his mother's birthday. After what she had said to him about his gift killing Morgan, buying her a gift for her birthday was just out of the question. He wanted to get as far away from New Salem as he could. The Army recruiter in Uniontown was all too happy to sign the boys up. They did their basic training together, and were allowed to do their stint in the Army together as well. While in basic training they were issued their gear, being part of Pershing's Doughboys. They received their campaign hat, tunic, cartridge belt, first aid pouch, rifle, bayonet, meat can pouch, entrenching tool, haversack, shelter tent, blanket roll, water canteen, breeches, leggings, and service shoes.

They were both used to the physical aspect of basic training, having worked the mines. Orville especially enjoyed mess. It was the best food he had ever eaten on a regular basis. They were quickly trained and dispatched to Europe. Orville and Geraint were eager to see Paris, but they were not nearly as thrilled as the French were to see them. Their unit marched through the streets of Paris on July 4, 1917. They were treated like celebrities by the Parisians. The French were war weary and tired of fighting off the German occupation. As the soldiers marched through the streets, the French people that remained in Paris came out to greet them. In their excitement, they threw cigarettes and candy to the soldiers to show their appreciation for their arrival. You could not have wiped the grins off Orville and Geraint's faces with a trowel full of cement. It was the best day of each of their lives and they both thought, if they died that very day, they would die happy. They felt that the two of them joining the

Army was the best decision they had ever made. As they marched through Paris, an American officer shouted out to the French people, "Nous voici, Lafayette!" interpreted, "Lafayette, we are here!" The French went mad with exuberance.

General John J. Pershing had a major disagreement with the British and French over their plan to split the American forces up and use them as reinforcements only. General Pershing was there to win the war and not to have his Army used as second-string players. He insisted that the Americans would fight united or they would not fight at all. He had no intentions of having his men spread out among the Allied Forces. The Doughboys sang George M. Cohan's song as they marched towards the trenches:

> Over there, over there
> Send the word, send the word, over there
> that the Yanks are coming,
> the yanks are coming,
> and we won't be back
> till it's over, over there.

Paris was still a beautiful city, even after the barrage of artillery that she had endured during the war. Many of the buildings were in ruin, and the streets had military debris everywhere. Just the same, Orville and Geraint enjoyed seeing Paris. Their outfit was now ordered to the western front. It was still in France, but it was a far cry from the likes of Paris. They hadn't seen much enemy movement as yet, but they were well aware that they needed to be mindful of their surroundings. They had marched through an area where the Germans left booby traps in the field. They hadn't discovered them until one buck private crossed a tripwire. He was the unit's first casualty of war. All that Orville and Geraint knew about the young man was that he was from Brooklyn, New York and his last name was Romanelli. The outfit called him Romie.

The clouds opened up and it began to gently rain. The rhythm of the droplets tapped against their helmets as they marched through France. Both the Americans and the British referred to their helmets as tin hats. The ground beneath them turned to muck as the massive army marched to their destination. The soldiers leading the way to the front were ordered that if the field had become too muddy for the rest of the unit to march through, they would have to begin laying duckboard for the army that was to follow. There were no roads to speak of, and so traffic jams happened frequently as great armies converged. It was still raining when the outfit saw the extended trench that, as far as they knew, would be their home away from home until the end of the war. It stretched as far as the eye could see. Between the Allied front and the German front lay no-man's land which was a vast wasteland of small knolls with dead vegetation sticking up, waving in the breeze as though there was some life left in their stalks. The Great War, as it was called, was simply referred to as a war of attrition, each side trying its best to wear the other side down. Geraint and Orville were getting ready to sit down and eat when they heard, "Mail call." Neither of them bothered to get up from their tin of slum, which was a thin stew the American soldiers often ate. Neither of them had received mail since they enlisted.

"Mayer, Stark, Catz, Bishop, Billings, Jenkins, Nevans. Hey Jenkins, you deaf? Get your mail, private," he called to Orville.

Orville threw his slum aside, jumped up and grabbed his letter. He could barely read, being illiterate, but he made out that it was from Kelly. He held the letter for a minute and looked around for a place where he could try and read it in private, but it was impossible to find a quiet spot in the middle of a war. He carefully opened the letter and attempted to read it; he soon realized that he needed some help. He went back and sat next to his friend with the letter.

"Who's the letter from?" Geraint asked.

"Kelly Hennessy," Orville said with a mischievous grin on his face.

"You're joking!" gasped Geraint.

"No, I'm pretty sure. Hey Evans, could you help me out and read it to me?" Orville asked.

"Oh yeah, are you kidding, I can't wait to see what this is about," Geraint said, excited for some news about home.

"Before you read this, you gotta promise you won't tell anyone," Orville demanded.

"Hey, this'll be between you and me, yah dog," Geraint swore.

Orville handed him the letter. When Geraint put out his hand to take it, Orville repeated, "Promise."

Geraint raised his right hand, "I swear, mate."

They sat down and Geraint looked the letter over before opening it. "Well you're right; it's from Kelly, postmarked Detroit, Michigan."

"Just open it," Orville said impatiently.

"Hey, keep your britches on. You act like we're in the middle of a war or something," Geraint teased.

"Yeah, real funny, just open the damn letter," Orville insisted.

"All right, if you're sure you want me to read this," Geraint asked.

"I'm sure," Orville confirmed.

Geraint began reading, "My dearest Orville."

Geraint paused for a moment, "My dearest Orville?... Are you sure you want me to read this?"

"Yeah, hurry up and go on," Orville said.

"I'm sorry this letter took so long to find you. I wrote to you in New Salem, but the letter was returned unopened. My sister Ann wrote to tell me that you and Geraint ran off and joined the Army. I hope this letter finds you. So much has happened. My father sent me away before I could tell you the news. I was scared at first, but now I'm glad to be here. I'm living with my aunt and uncle in Detroit. They have a huge home, plenty of room for me and the baby," Kelly wrote. Geraint stopped reading and looked at Orville. "Me and the baby? What the hell is she talking about?" Orville shrugged his shoulders, and shook his head, "I have no idea."

She went on to write, "I never had the chance to tell you about our baby."

Geraint stopped once more, blurting out, "OUR BABY? You dog."

"Are you joking me? Did she really say that?" Orville questioned.

"No fooling, I'm reading this, word for word,"

Geraint said, assuring his friend.

Orville's jaw gaped open as Geraint read the rest of her letter.

"I hope you don't mind, but when I had a baby boy, I named him Morgan Joseph."

"Well I'll be damned," was Geraint's response to the information.

Orville was still too shocked to speak. Geraint went on to read, "I pray you're safe and well. When you come home we can get married and live here in Detroit, if that's all right with you. I'll write soon." She signed the letter, "All my love, Kelly."

Geraint and Orville simply stared at each other, being left dumbfounded. Neither of them had anything to say about Kelly's letter. They were both still in shock by what Geraint had just read. The silence was quickly interrupted by a barrage of German artillery, but no matter how large the shells were that were going off all around them, they were nothing compared to the bomb that Kelly had just dropped on them.

Between battles were long hours where much of the time was devoted to picking lice out of the seams of clothes. The soldiers referred to body lice as chats, and the process of removing them was called chatting. The trenches were a breeding ground for all sorts of nasty problems. It rained so often that the soldiers stood and fought in mud and muck. The duckboard helped, but it could only do so much. The medics kept busy treating everything from trench mouth to trench foot to trench fever. Another common infestation in the trenches was a blood-sucking vermin the men called cooties. In fact, a buck private named McCollum

of the 77th Division wrote a poem that became popular. His
poem went as follows:

"COOTIES"
When you're standing at attention,
and the cooties duck below;
just the way they come for seconds,
ain't it hell? Well, I'll say so!
In the lines the boys were diggin'
with their shovels to get in,
while the cootie rigged his digger
with his rig for diggin' in.
At the front the majors had'em;
every captain raised his share,
but there sure was Hell a-poppin'
when a buck had one to spare.
Each and every nation has them,
both the great ones and the small;
but for the tame and naughty cooties
rainy France, she leads them all.

Orville corresponded with Kelly as often as the war
would allow. He registered her name with the military as next
of kin and awarded her his benefits. Since Kelly was now living in Detroit, Orville thought that it would be nice if she could
find out what had happened to his older brother Bill. Bill was
Orville's best friend until the fight between him and their father
drove him away for good. The last that Orville had heard about
his brother was that he had taken a job in the steelworks and
was living somewhere in Detroit. Orville really missed Bill and
thought that he would enjoy meeting with Kelly and his son,
Morgan. Orville knew that Bill would be more than willing to
help out until he came home from the war. Geraint began writing his family, too, but never revealed anything about what was
going on between Orville and Kelly. His father would write back
and let him know all the news from home.

Every letter that his father wrote to him started the same way. He would convey that everyone was doing well except, and then he would proceed to list everyone's name from the local obituary. Geraint was homesick; he missed his father's sense of humor and everyone he left behind. His father wrote to Geraint that Dafydd and Ann were going to marry and Dafydd was now working with him in the mines. He wrote and told him how big Catherine was getting, but he failed to mention much about how his mother was doing. Geraint figured that she must still be angry with him about, in her way of thinking, killing Morgan and going off to war. Orville was anxious to see his fiancée as well as his son and hoped to see his brother Bill again. Orville often dreamt of the grand reunion they would have when he came home. He finally had someone he could call his own. He and Geraint would talk while they "chatted".

Word came through their first December in France that the Russians signed an armistice with Germany, following the success of the Bolsheviks Revolution. The terms of the treaty were made known through out the military because of the harshness of the concessions. Russia had to surrender the Ukraine, Poland, as well as a few other regions as part of the agreement. Russia also agreed to stop all propaganda against Germany and was fined 300 million rubles for repatriation of Russian prisoners.

The war dragged on as casualties mounted. There was now a new fear, which had nothing to do with the war. There was a pandemic of flu called The Spanish Lady which had spread throughout the world. It was a respiratory infection that was indiscriminately killing millions of people. It was a quick but painful death. The onset of flu symptoms was a high fever accompanied by severe headaches. Those who were infected had lips that turned a sickly blue color as their lungs filled with fluids, making it difficult to breath. Within a few days of the blue discoloring of the mouth, most of those who were infected drowned because of the fluid build-up causing them to suffocate. It was a horrible death. By the time the flu ran its course, no fewer than

20 million people died and as many as 50 million would suc-
cumb to its lethal blow worldwide.

In cities around the world, undertakers were traveling up
and down roads asking the living to bring out the dead. Millions
in the military were affected and transported the dreaded disease
across the world as they were released from duty. Geraint and
Orville, or Evans and Jenkins, as all the soldiers were known
by last names only, had long since discovered that enlisting in
the war was not the answer to their problems like they had both
thought. The new strain of flu was killing as many soldiers as
the Germans were. They were tired of living in filth, and being
around all of the death and dying. They had witnessed more
men, both German and allies, blown to bits than they could
count. They witnessed for themselves the horrors of what mus-
tard gas could do to a man, and now the flu was killing soldiers
by the droves. Every day they wondered if they would live, die,
or just be maimed. They wanted to go home and see their families; they wanted their lives back.

The soldiers never knew when the Germans would come
over the top with their potato mashers, rifles and bayonets. The
Allies inevitably pushed them back again. Back and forth the
soldiers moved across no-man's land from the Allied trenches to
the enemies trenches, continually. They rarely saw a brass hat,
which was what the low-ranking soldiers called a high-ranking
officer, but they knew when one had been in touch with their
sergeant. The word coming down the pike was that there would
be a new attack against the Germans. It was very hush, hush and
called the Big Show, or the Meuse-Argonne Offensive. D-Day
was to be September 25, 1918, but zero hour was 5:30 a.m. on
the 26th.

The men steadied themselves for the big push into the
German occupied territory of France and Belgium.

General Pershing was head of operations. Nine divisions were to lead in the attack. They were to be deployed from
the Meuse River on the east to the rim of the Argonne Forest to the west. The right side of the offensive was to be held

by Major General Bullard and his three divisions of infantry. On the left side was Major General Leggett commanding his army of men. In the center position, which was the thrust of the attack, stood Major General Cameron overseeing the soldiers in his command. Each major general had three divisions with one division in reserve. It was a massive operation; there were nearly three thousand machine guns as well as cannons for firing the heavier artillery which the soldiers referred to as Jack Johnson's. One big advantage was the Allies were to deploy nearly two hundred tanks into the mission to which the German army had none. There would be over eight hundred of our airplanes to support the attack of the infantry. We had, by far, the superior army.

The Fourth Army of the French was to advance west of the Argonne Forest, forcing the German army to evacuate the woods and rush towards a hornet's nest of artillery that was waiting for them. The battle was fierce. For the first few days of the offensive, allied troops advanced steadily. A few hours prior to the Germans getting their reinforcements, the Allies took Montfaucon by noon on the second day of the battle. The Germans had gathered a powerful machine gun defense supported by heavy artillery fire. The center corps under Major General Cameron sustained an enormous amount of casualties from the heavy crossfire they were under. The Allies had advanced farther, taking Baulny, Epinonville, Septsarges, and Dannevoux.

On the far left, the Germans were striking powerful blows and made frequent counter attacks with their fresh troops. Towards evening on the 29th, the soldiers dug in. As the sun went down, a heavy fog rolled in wearing on our soldiers' minds. They listened to the whiz-bangs flying overhead and waited for the explosion hoping one didn't find their position. As the soldiers put it, they were up against the wall. The communication wires that ran across no-man's land had been severed. The treacherous bombardment of shells had virtually destroyed radio contact for our troops. They had to fight blind until communications could be restored which was a top priority for the troops. Phase two of the Meuse-Argonne offensive began at 5:30 a.m. on the 4th of

October. The Germans had a commanding position on the heights east of the Meuse. They had established a machine gun nest from a vantage point directly in our immediate front. The Allies were ordered to wear them down and take the position. They tried to outflank the Germans by launching a strong attack on their less-defended side, causing them to shift their priorities to one that was beneficial to the Allies. Besides their own replacements, the Allies still had four divisions they could count on; two were British and two were French.

In early October, their combat units required nearly 90,000 replacements for weary units. At that rate they would only have 45,000 replacements left for the fighting if it continued into November. It was a critical situation, causing the fighting infantry to be pushed to their limits and beyond. The First Army was maintaining their hold on over 120 kilometers of the frontline. They were about one million men strong and really too large an area for one commander, even with a staff, to defend. But, defend they did. The war seemed to intensify as they were fast approaching the eleventh hour. The fatigue from the continual battles took their toll on the soldiers. The battle would continue into yet another month. The fighting men were exhausted. Combat troops held the line against insurmountable odds, their fortitude being pushed to the limits day after day. The Germans were reduced to engaging in crisis situations without resources that were critical to their success. This brought the German morale to an all-time low.

The Third Phase of the Meuse-Argonne, or the Big Show, was to be set in motion. General Pershing intended to stand and fight until victory was assured. The First Army was called on again by the brass hats to get ready for a general attack. They had seven days to prepare before their next offensive. Jenkins and Evans and the remaining men of the outfit prepared, knowing they would be meeting fierce resistance from the Germans and may not make it out alive. It was a do-or-die situation for both sides and it was to be a decisive battle. It was planned that the Fourth French Army would be at their left. They coordinated the attack simultaneously; D-Day for the Third Phase would be November 1. The orders sent down to the First Army were to take Buzancy and the heights around Barricourt and to establish communications with the Fourth French Army near Boult-aux-Bois. The orders were then to drive through towards Sedan. The big guns along with our tanks were in position to support the infantry's attack. All three Army corps were in line at the newly established front, which ran from the river to Bois de Bourgogne. The Fifth Division was commissioned to build a bridge across the Meuse River. Everything was in position from the communication lines to water service for the troops.

The infantry advanced with the support from the tanks and accompanying guns. The strategy of the battle was organized and well thought out. They were able to advance farther than planned. They completed the capture of the heights and Bois de Folie. On November 2nd and 3rd, Jenkins and Evans's division advanced quickly across country roads, destroying the Carignan-Sedan Railroad, at Longuyon and Conflan junction which transported supplies to the German army. On the 4th of November, Jenkins and Evans's division advanced to Beaumont. The First Army was then directed to take Longwy. Private Jenkins ran ahead of the rest of the unit yelling for the men to hurry. As the unit caught up with Jenkins, a fierce gun battle ensued.

"Dig in, boys!" The order rang out through the unit. They held their position long enough to wear the war- weary Germans down. The unit began to advance again. The Germans were on the run. The First Army was chasing the Germans down. Private Madera was next to Jenkins and Evans when he hit a tripwire. Jenkins continued to fire his weapon until all of his ammo was used. He killed four Germans who turned and fired upon them after they were wounded by the explosion. The land mine killed Madera outright. Jenkins and Evans were both wounded by it and couldn't go on. They were transported to the hospital. Orville was unconscious and had lost a lot of blood; the battle continued without them. Geraint had non life-threatening injuries throughout the left side of his body.

Both men needed surgery. Orville woke with Geraint in the next bed. Geraint knew, by the way the nurses talked while Orville was still under the anesthetic that his friend was in really bad shape. The buck private in charge of mail call brought a letter over and sat it on Jenkins's cot. Orville had one eye wrapped with gauze; he asked the nurse to give the letter to Geraint in the next bed, which she did without question. Geraint looked at the letter. It was from Detroit, but he thought it was odd because he did not recognize the handwriting on the envelope. He had read enough letters from Kelly to know that she had not written this one.

He opened and quickly scanned through the letter, understanding the content. Geraint made the excuse that he was really tired and if Orville didn't mind, he would read it to him later. Orville agreed, being sore and tired himself. Geraint rolled over, turning his back towards Orville and quietly reopened the letter while his friend rested. The letter was from Kelly's Aunt Ruby. Geraint's heart sank in his chest as he read it. She was writing to inform Orville that Kelly had died October 28th of the flu. Kelly's Aunt Ruby went on to write that she wanted Orville to come get his son as soon as the war was over, or she would have no choice but to place the boy in an orphanage. Geraint watched as Orville restlessly moved around in his sleep and wished he could get out of adding insult to injury. He knew the news about Kelly's dying would devastate him; he often talked about how badly he wanted to see her as well as his son. Orville's condition had already been deemed critical, and Geraint overheard the nurses talk as though his friend might not make it. Geraint was unsure what he should do. He felt that if the shoe was on the other foot, he would want to know, if only to set up some kind of living arrangement for his son. He knew that if Orville did die, he surely would not want his son ending up in an orphanage.

Orville moaned as he awoke from his sleep. Sgt. Hawkens entered the ward and approached Orville's cot. They presented him with two medals. One was the Purple Heart while the other, even more prestigious, was the Medal of Honor.

Sgt. Hawkens read the citation to Private Jenkins. It read, "After his platoon had gained its objective, PFC Jenkins courageously, after being wounded by a land mine, continued discharging his weapon until all ammo was used, killing four German soldiers." Private Jenkins acknowledged his accomplishment with a sigh. He was in far too much pain to fully comprehend the honor being bestowed upon him. Sgt. Hawkens moved to the next cot. Geraint was also awarded the Purple Heart for being wounded in action. After the presentation, Geraint closed his eyes, pretending as though he was asleep. He hoped that Orville would do the same. Geraint needed time to compose himself enough to tell Orville what had happened to all his dreams.

Orville did drift off for a few minutes. As he woke, he believed that Geraint was asleep. Orville did not think about the medals; his thoughts were on the letter that was tucked under Geraint's pillow. Just a corner of the envelope was visible. Orville hoped that the letter had something to do with Kelly finding out where his brother Bill lived.

"I bet Bill can get me into the steelworks," Orville thought within himself.

Orville waited until a nurse walked by. "Umm... Excuse me, do you think you could read me that letter over there?" he said pointing at Geraint's cot. "It's mine, but I can't read it because of the injury to my eyes; everything is blurry," he claimed.

Geraint was listening to everything and as the nurse reached for the letter, Geraint opened his eyes while holding onto it. He explained that he was awake and would be able to read it to his friend after all. He was shaking as he pulled the letter out of the envelope. He stared at it trying to figure out how he should tell him. Geraint wanted desperately to spare Orville hearing what he was about to tell him. He couldn't think of a way around it and Orville was growing impatient.

"Quit stalling and read it. What, Kelly can't find Bill?" Orville questioned.

"No, it has nothing to do with Bill." Geraint took a deep sigh, wishing the news was something as unimportant as that.

Geraint swallowed and warned his friend, "Brace yourself. This is bad, bad news."

As Geraint read the letter aloud to Orville, a deep penetrating cry was heard throughout the hospital. Several nurses rushed over to see what was wrong and to help him through his pain. Not even morphine could help his suffering now. Telling Orville about Kelly was, by far, the hardest thing that Geraint had ever done. He hated being the bearer of the horrible news. His only consolation was that he had hoped that it was somehow better hearing what had happened to Kelly from a friend, who cared and knew her, rather than hearing it from a nurse who, in all respects, was a stranger. The nurses rushed over to sedate Orville. It took two of them to hold him down as one administered the shot that with in a few minutes would render him unconscious. Later that same day came the announcement everyone was waiting for. The war was over. As Geraint heard the news and began to cry, he ached knowing how close his lifelong friend had come to having all of his dreams come true. And now, everything he had was shattered into a million pieces that could never be put together again.

The nurses thought he was crying for joy with them. It was strange; it was partly that, but mostly he cried out of sympathy for Kelly and Orville. The doctors, nurses, and patients rejoiced together. Those that could move jumped around the ward, hugging and kissing each other. The exuberance throughout the entire hospital could not be quenched. Orville was still under heavy sedation and was completely unaware that the war had ended. Orville slept for over twelve hours after he was administered his shot. It was quiet in the hospital when Orville awoke from his sleep. Geraint heard him stirring and asked him if he was all right. He told Orville the good news about the war being over and that they would be shipped home soon. Orville just lay there unaffected by the news. He did not believe that he was going home; he had no one to go home to anymore. Once Orville regained his composure, he discussed with Geraint what he thought would be best for his son. He told Geraint what he wanted him to do if he didn't make it home. Orville asked Geraint if he thought that his parents would raise his son. He didn't want Kelly's father involved with his upbringing at all. He expressed to Geraint how happy he was the day he went to his house for dinner and they looked through his father's scrapbook. He told Geraint that he considered that to be the best memory he had growing up, and he wanted his son to experience a home with that kind of love in it too.

Orville looked over at Geraint and, with all sincerity, asked, "Do you think there's a heaven?"

"Sure there is," Geraint told him with confidence.

"Do you think I'll make it in?" Orville asked, believing that he had fallen short.

"Without a doubt, mate," Geraint assured him.

Orville began to cry again. "I sure hope you're right; maybe I'll see Kelly there?"

"Ah, don't talk like that. You'll be fine. I'll go to Detroit with you and we'll get your son. My God, Orville, he's over a year old already," Geraint said hoping to encourage him.

"Yeah, and I haven't even seen a picture of him... God I'd like to be with him when he grows up. Make sure you tell that boy that I loved him. It's important for a boy to know that his father loved him. I wish I'd have had an old man that loved me. Maybe things would have been different. Promise me you will give him my medals. Maybe Morgan will believe that I really was brave and not some kind of a bum," Orville confessed.

"Ah, stop talking like that. Everything will be all right. Why don't you get some rest," Geraint pleaded.

A few days passed by while an infection reeked havoc on Orville's body. The doctors and nurses did all they could for him. They told Geraint that once someone loses his will to fight, there really is not much that can be done. They would have to wait and see. Orville drifted in and out of consciousness as Geraint looked on and prayed. He felt guilty about how strong he was feeling, knowing his friend was dying. He knew he would be released from the hospital within a few days.

They did their duty and their mission was a success. Geraint watched as Orville became delirious and spoke of some of the battles as though he were back there again. He was not making much sense when suddenly, as clear and lucid as he ever was, he stretched out his hand and said, "Ah, Kelly, let's go over by that stream and sit for a while," and with that Orville died, seemingly peaceful and smiling. Geraint decided that Orville should be buried in France.

It was a cold, foggy morning as Geraint left the hospital in search of his friend's final resting place. The clouds appeared full, gray and heavy with rain. A stiff breeze chilled the air, chasing the fog away. Geraint, with the aid of his crutches as well as one of his attending nurses, went to the cemetery just outside Paris. As they approached the site, the clouds opened and a soft cold shower washed over them. A simple white cross read: "PFC Orville Jenkins. Died Nov. 14,1918." It was a somber occasion. Geraint placed some flowers that he brought with him from the hospital in front of Orville's cross. The mound of fresh soil was quickly becoming saturated by the rain turning to mud. Geraint respectively saluted the cross. He turned to the nurse and said he was ready to leave. She escorted him back to the army hospital where he made his preparations to return to America.

He carefully packed his and Orville's belongings for the trip home. Geraint was discharged from the hospital and sent home December 20th. Geraint was anxious to return; he did, however, make one stop in Detroit before going home to New Salem. He was determined to make everything work out the way Orville wanted it to. He would do everything in his power to honor his friend's last request. As soon as Geraint made it to Detroit and saw Orville's son, his eyes welted up with tears. Morgan was the very image of his father. Geraint thought of how proud Orville would have been to see the lad. Geraint was determined that this boy would have a good life, and would grow up with people that loved him. There was much to think about as he and Orville's son made the trip back to Pennsylvania. He was certain that as soon as his mother laid eyes on the child and heard his name, her heart would melt. He could not imagine that she would deny a dying soldier's last request, even if it was Orville Jenkins. If she did, however, he thought of a backup plan.

Geraint considered Dafydd and Ann as being a candidate to possibly raise Morgan as their own. He was Ann's nephew, after all. Geraint's only concern was the Hennessys. He wondered what they would say about his family raising their grandson. Catherine Hennessy was still grieving over the loss of her daughter. She, too, had received the horrible news from Aunt Ruby about Kelly's tragic death. She also now knew who the father of the baby was as well as the child's name. Aunt Ruby had written Cate telling her that Orville would be picking the child up as soon as he was home from the war, but she had no idea where they would settle. Sean insisted that Kelly be buried in Detroit. The only people present at the funeral were her aunt and uncle. Catherine was not allowed to go; she needed to stay and take care of her husband. She bore feelings of shame, embarrassment, and curiosity about her grandson. She wondered if she would ever be allowed to see his face.

Just before Kelly gave birth to the baby, her father Sean had been in a serious mining accident. He and three other miners were pinned under a broken brace beam and some heavy rocks. The area of the shaft where they were trapped quickly filled with water. The three miners near him died. One drowned not having the strength to keep his head above water because of his injuries. The other two were killed outright by the explosion that caused the cave-in. Their lifeless bodies seemed to reach out to Sean as they floated face down in the water. He sat there and waited for his turn to die. It was hours before the rescue and recovery was completed. The miners worked tirelessly, knowing four of their own were trapped. Sean Hennessy was the only one still alive by the time the trapped miners were reached. His legs had been ravished by the accident and he would never be able to walk again. The Black Maria transported him to the hospital where the doctors examined him extensively. They consulted one another and determined that because tiny slivers of coal and wood remained inside him, gangrene would be eminent and both of his legs would have to come off. Mr. Hennessy was informed of the grave situation that he was in. He nearly refused the surgery, but decided he would rather live than die.

A few weeks after the amputations, Sean Hennessy was transported home for his wife to attend his needs. Sean's bitterness grew after the surgery. Kelly never knew what had happened to her father. The Hennessys managed to keep the accident a secret for over a year. Sean had threatened Ann and Catherine to keep quiet. He did not want Kelly to think that she could come back into their life to help. He was adamant that he would never allow her or her baby back. Catherine was no longer afraid of her husband like she had been in the past. The mining accident drained him of most of his strength. There was not much he could do except yell at her and call her names. Whenever he would start she would simply leave the room. Once in a while if he was really frustrated he would throw something at her. He never did let up on Kelly for having a baby out of wedlock, even though she was gone. He still blamed Catherine for everything that had gone wrong within the family.

He often told her that no "bastard", as long as he was alive, would ever live under "his roof."

Her thought was that she was already living with a bastard.

Sean told Catherine as soon as he found out that Orville might be picking the boy up, "He best keep that little bastard in Detroit, because he is not welcomed here."

Cate warned him, "If you ever call my grandson a bastard again I'll kill you."

He threw a glass bottle that was in his hand at her, but it hit the wall instead.

"Ah, you missed again. I guess even your aim isn't what it used to be," she told him as she left the room After the crippling mining accident, Sean was more cantankerous than ever. Cate continued to put up with all of his guff. The two of them fought continually. It broke her heart knowing she would never be allowed to have her grandson over to their home while Sean was alive; she wouldn't want him to be subjected to his abuse anyhow. At first she thought it would be best if he did not come around at all, but she became ashamed of herself for being so selfish.

Geraint arrived in New Salem on a brisk January evening with little Morgan Jenkins. Geraint was glad to be home again. As he walked home from the bus depot, he pointed out the lot where the old Jenkins house used to be, even though he knew Morgan was too young to understand what he was talking about. As Geraint approached his family's home, he reflected on everything that had transpired. Morgan was quiet as a church mouse. The only sound that Geraint heard was the sound of his own footsteps crunching in the snow. He considered how ironic it was that the last January he was home, they had buried his brother Morgan. This January he was returning with another. He hoped that this would be his redemption. As he approached the front steps to his parents' house, he took a deep breath and walked up to the door with Orville's son bundled up and straddled on his shoulders. Geraint carried the child just as his father used to carry their Morgan when he was small. He knocked at the door instead of just walking in. His mother opened it thinking it was Cate coming over because of the fight she had just had with Sean. She nearly fainted when she saw who was standing just outside her door. She could hardly speak for a second. She pulled them inside and called to the family out of joy.

Mari had never been so glad to see someone in her life. Geraint was right about one thing. She melted when she saw the child, and she began to weep when he told her his name. He explained why he brought him to them. He told his parents that this was a dying soldier's last request and how much it had meant to him. He told his mother and father what Orville had said about the day he was invited over and how he said that it was the best day of his life. He also said how brave Orville was while he was under fire. Geraint showed his mother and father the medals that Orville had been presented along with the citation explaining the reason he was awarded them.

Mari's heart swelled with guilt when she heard about how much that day had meant to Orville and how unfair she had been to him. They quickly agreed to raise the child as their own. He would now be known as Morgan Joseph Evans II, not to replace their Morgan; nothing or no one could do that. They decided they could not let that sweet little boy go into an orphanage. Cate had overcome her pride as soon as she laid eyes on the child. He did look like Orville, but Cate could see Kelly in him also. She was grateful for the Evans's decision to take the boy into their home and raise him as their own. She knew that he would be well looked after. She loved the fact that she would be able to watch her grandson grow up in spite of her husband. Even Sean Hennessy could not control what his neighbors did. Cate's intent was to keep Morgan as far away from his grandfather as she could. She felt that it would not be that hard of a task considering the state he was in. For the first time in her life she felt that she was in complete control, and it felt wonderful.

Mari and Cate doted over the child. He was their joy and their life. Morgan Joseph Evans II grew up healthy and happy. He was told about his mother, his father and his father's sacrifice and the great love they he had for him, as promised. He also knew about the great love that his father and mother had for each other. He grew to become a handsome young man that was loved by everyone. When he was to wed, his adoptive mother, Mari, presented him some gifts just prior to his wedding: her mother's wedding ring which Morgan gave to his bride with great pride. On that very day, he was also given his father's Medal of Honor and his Purple Heart.

THE END

22729206R00087

Made in the USA
Charleston, SC
01 October 2013